Four tawdry tales will delight your senses and leave you deeply satisfied.

LOGGER'S DELIGHT
Doug Hayburn is a timberbeast who prefers to stay away from the prying eyes and taunting jeers of men. His colossal member attracts too much attention. When Logan Pettigrew, a logger with quite the opposite problem, arrives on the scene, he proves that Love always has the last laugh.

KWIKLUBE 5000
Jack "Snake" Elgin is a businessman who sought to capitalize on the explosion in car culture in Los Angeles. He battles inner demons and outer extremities. His employees help release him from a personal hell into a new kind of heaven.

HOTSHOT
Hugh Jayness inherited a large pickup truck from his stepfather and a tiny member from his father. He loves hanging out at truck stops, giving truckers the satisfaction they crave. After reading a want-ad, Hugh realizes he can join the world of hotshot trucking.

FIREHOUSE LOVERS
Travis Baumholt knows he's gay, but he's not comfortable with it, Given his small member, big ass, and remarkable talents, he isn't sure where he fits in. Enter Mike, a massive man with a huge problem only Travis can solve.

HOT BLUE COLLARS

Workplace Encounters

PETER SCHUTES

CONTENTS

FOREWORD

LOGGER'S DELIGHT - A logger chooses to live away from society, out in the woods, with only a bunch of men and some halfway decent food to keep him company. Some loggers are loners, preferring to live and work away from others. These 'timberbeasts' always have good reasons for wishing to be alone. Some are hotheads who would get in fights if they were around others. Others are introverted types who feel drained by other people. Some of these solitary loggers have reasons no one could fathom.

Doug Hayburn, the protagonist of our story, preferred to stay away from the prying eyes and taunting jeers of men. His massive member attracted too much attention. He couldn't shower, dine, or work among the men without the damn thing getting in the way. Men were envious, lustful, and cruel. He chose the life of a timberbeast because it was the only way he could find peace and earn a living away from society. Can anything tame the wild timberbeast? Love could if he would allow himself to risk being hurt. Doug was once made a fool in love and wished never to love again. When Logan Pettigrew, a logger with quite the opposite problem, arrives on the scene, he proves that Fate always has the last laugh.

KWIKLUBE 5000, a long short story, takes place on Van Nuys Boulevard in the San Fernando Valley of Los Angeles in the 1970s. At that time, Van Nuys was the "cruising" street of choice for young drivers. Cruising was outlawed by the quasi-fascist LAPD, who saw fit to curtail freedoms if they were inconvenient, for along with the cruising came fights, accidents, and crime. Jack "Snake" Elgin is a businessman who sought to capitalize on the explosion in car culture in his hometown. This story tells a tale of a man battling inner demons and outer extremities. His employees help bring him out of his own personal hell into a new kind of heaven.

Of this Story, Peter wrote: KwikLube 5000 was my first attempt at portraying the San Fernando Valley, the capital of pornography and bleach blond hair. The Valley is an enigmatic place. There is no "there" there, as Gertrude Stein would say. It's just an endless expanse of ugly signs and drive-thru businesses. Nobody leaves his or her car, which is why KwikLube 5000 was such a success. The driver could stay in the car and read the Los Angeles Times while mechanics fiddled with the car one story down. Despite my disparaging words, the Valley is dear to my heart. The bathhouses there have the most handsome men, who are much more receptive to an old, well-hung fart like me.

HOTSHOT — In the 1960s, a new kind of trucking arose. Hotshot trucking is when a man owns a pickup truck and modifies it for use on short-haul, small-payload runs. These Hotshots are nimble and quick. When something has to be there overnight, they are a fast solution to supply chain issues. They are still in demand today, especially in oil country, where parts must arrive lickety-split to keep the derricks running.

Hugh Jayness, the story's protagonist, inherited a large pickup truck from his stepfather and a tiny penis from his father. He loved hanging out at truck stops, giving truckers the satisfaction they crave. After reading a want-ad, Hugh realizes he can not just inhabit the trucker's world; he can join it.

FIREHOUSE LOVERS —Many gay men are excited by the heroism and bravery of our nation's fire brigades. It doesn't hurt that they are masculine, muscular, and usually quite handsome. These men work in 24-hour tours that begin at 8:00 am every day. They will have one day on and one or two days off. The shifts are coordinated so that the team is consistent. Nobody from one team ever works with another. This promotes a strong sense of camaraderie. While most firefighters return to a wife and kids, a strong contingent of men prefer a solitary life. They don't want a woman with children worrying about losing them, but more importantly, they choose the company of men. These rugged heroes must be prepared to drop everything when a call comes in.

Travis Baumholt knows he's gay, but he's not comfortable with it, even though he lives in the heart of the Castro District in San Francisco, which, even in the late 1960s, was becoming a mecca for gay men. Little by little, he is discovering who he is and where he belongs on the hierarchy of gay sex. Given his small member, big ass, and remarkable talents, he seems most satisfied as Greek passive, French active. Enter Mike, a massive man with a huge problem only Travis can solve.

❄ I ❄
LOGGER'S DELIGHT

THE TIMBERBEAST

Doug Hayburn was a timberbeast, a long-logger who was too wild to live in the bunkhouse with the rest of the crew. He felled giant fir trees with just an ax and a rope. The others worked as a team, bringing down ten firs a day between the seven of them. Doug took down three trees a day by himself. So, the company left him to his wild, loner ways. He lived in a tent a long way from camp. He bathed in the icy river out of sight of the others.

Doug had a secret. Under his loose overalls, between his legs, lurked a boa constrictor-sized piece of meat. He lived apart from other men because it had a terrible effect on them. For as long as he could remember, men humiliated him for his size. In high school, the football players neighed like horses when he walked by. He stopped showering in the gym, but it was too late. His reputation was out there. Doe-eyed cheerleaders and queer football players cornered him in the hallways begging him to be with them, but he knew it was useless. He'd tried a few times without any luck. Nobody could even begin to take him. His magnificent organ sowed the seeds of his loneliness. So he spilled his seed alone.

When Doug graduated high school, the life of a logger called to him. He yearned to be away from the trappings of society among men who didn't give a hoot. It turned out that most of them did give a hoot. They were more down to earth than the assholes in high school, but they were still mesmerized by his massive endowment. When he showered with the logging crew, all heads turned to his crotch. He hated the attention. He was tempted to quit that first day but stuck around to learn the ropes. The food was terrible. But it was there in the camp he met a timberbeast named Stew.

Stew lived apart from the camp and worked alone. When he arrived at camp, Doug was young and scrawny; Stew took him under his wing and taught him how to work alone. Stew kept away for the same reason as Doug; he, too, was massive.

The two men collected their supper in the cookhouse and brought it back to Stew's tent, where they ate around the campfire.

"Stew, why do you think God made us like this?"

The older man rubbed his chin. "Well, Doug, it was a pretty mean joke, that's for sure. Everybody I know wishes they were bigger. Everyone except you and me. It's ironic."

Doug nodded. "Yeah, but I mean, why? Why play a joke on us?"

Stew put an arm around the young man. Nestled in the man's huge embrace, Doug felt a tingling warmth in his crotch. Stew watched the boy's overalls tent upwards. Doug felt something move near his elbow. Stew's pole was straining against his dungarees.

"I'm sorry, sir. I can't help it." Doug blushed.

Stew smiled. "I can. Let's help each other."

The two men released the giants in their pants. Doug's was a hand higher than Stew's and bigger around.

The logger whistled. "Damn! That's one huge pecker pole."

When Stew put a rough hand on it, his fingers didn't touch. He used both hands to rub Doug's prize, and Doug returned the favor. Despite their enormous size, both men were quick to climax. Stew came first, drenching them both. When Doug came, to his surprise, Stew clamped his mouth over the opening and swallowed.

"What does it taste like?"

Stew stared. "You mean you've never swallowed another man's load?"

Doug shook his head.

Stew stood and slapped Doug's face with his meat. "Put your mouth on it, and you can find out for yourself. It tastes great."

Doug opened his mouth wide and covered the head of Stew's swelling member. He couldn't put the whole thing in, but he tried.

"Good. Now lick it and suck it."

Doug obliged. Stew's knees buckled. "Oh yeah. Oh, Doug! Damn!"

A trickle of precum salted his mouth. He got hard again. He held his own member to his chest and rubbed it while he sucked Stew. With his free hand, he jacked Stew's pole at the base.

"Yeah, just like that. Good boy. Keep sucking. Use your tongue."

Doug swirled his tongue around the tip, tasting the older man like an ice cream cone. He tasted great. The more he sucked, the harder he got. His fist flew up and down where the tip met his nipples.

Stew's knees shook hard. "Oh, Doug, I think I'm gonna come."

Doug ran his hand up and down Stew's massive thigh and felt his butt muscles clenching in preparation for orgasm. Stew held the boy's head still while he jerked off.

"Yeah!"

Doug felt a warm rush fill his mouth to overflowing. He swallowed, enjoying the strong flavor of man. He could swear his chest hair grew thick at that moment. It was so exciting he almost forgot he was masturbating. When he came, it hit his chin hard, surprising him. Stew put a thick finger under his chin, then licked it clean.

Doug set up camp next to Stew for the rest of the season. Every morning, they headed out to fell giant firs together. Every night, they gave each other pleasure. The rest of the logger camp talked about them in whispers whenever they entered the mess house. Neither man cared. They were an exclusive club with two giant members. Stew taught Doug the life of a timberbeast. When the first heavy snow came, the operations ceased. The season was over. The men went back to their homes.

Doug and Stew promised to meet at the camp when the next season began, but it didn't happen. Doug arrived, searching everywhere for his friend; a logger took him aside. "Stew got arrested in Salem; he ain't coming back."

Doug pitched his tent a half mile from camp so nobody would see him crying. He'd found the one man in the world who understood him. He missed the smell of his sweat. His heart broke. He was a lone timberbeast, as Stew had been. And so he stayed out there season after season. He went from a wiry young man to a massively muscled logger.

As the years passed, he forgot what it was like to have a companion. His beard was unkempt, and his eyes were wild. The whispers of the first summer were gone. Doug's huge secret passed out of common knowledge, replaced by rumors that he was not mentally well. The stories were partly true. But Doug was strong-willed. He learned to love the isolation of his tent away from the bunkhouse. The lonely logger still imagined what it would be like to hold another man close and kiss him like he had done that first season with Stew. Doug's life was solitary and unchanging; he never dreamed it would get better.

A NEW ARRIVAL

Doug's tenth season changed him. A cherubic newcomer named Logan Pettigrew arrived at camp. He was the whistle punk, the kid in charge of blowing the whistle to alert the team when to stop and start the motor that pulled the roped logs. It was an entry-level position, easily trained. Doug first saw Logan in the mess house the day he arrived. The other men were teasing him mercilessly. Doug shrugged. "He can figure it out himself like I did." But Doug felt guilty for failing to intervene.

A week later, the boy looked at Doug, the timber-beast with wild hair and matted beard, and smiled. Doug hadn't seen a smile in a decade. The boy motioned him over.

"Come sit next to me."

Doug hadn't eaten in the mess house since the day he met Stew, but he was so surprised that he just sat.

"I'm Logan Pettigrew, and you are...?"

"Doug. Doug Hayburn."

Doug took the outstretched hand, so soft and delicate. His own hand was easily three times the size.

"May I read your palm?"

This kid was nuts. Doug chuckled. "Knock yourself out."

Logan held the massive paw and traced the lines.

"The heart line appears broken, see?" He ran his little finger diagonally across Doug's hand. Sure enough, the line split.

"But see here? It joins with the life line; your heart will heal when you join your life with another."

Doug pulled his hand back. This kid was stirring up emotions he'd worked very hard to smother.

"Which job do you have? I'll bet you're a bucker."

Doug smiled. "I'm a timberbeast. A loner; I don't work with a team."

Logan stared into Doug's eyes. "I wonder why not. Why don't you like people?"

"People...want things. I don't want to talk about it."

Logan nodded. "I believe I know what you mean."

Doug doubted it. Judging by the kid's tiny hands, he would have no idea what Doug had to deal with.

Logan said, "Some of the guys here are not very nice."

Doug felt oddly protective of this cherubic youth. "What did they do? Who's been mean to you?"

Logan shook his head. "It's okay. They made fun of me in the showers when I got here. All of them."

Doug said, "Are you...?"

Logan nodded. "Tiny little dick. Yes. But it's none of their business."

"I, er, I get made fun of in the showers too."

Logan said, "Are you...?"

"Monster cock. Yep."

The air grew still. Doug sipped his black coffee. He noticed that Logan took cream and sugar. A few whispers and averted glances told the two that they were the subject of idle gossip.

"How small?"

Logan looked around. He formed the letter C with his thumb and index finger. "About that big. How about you?"

Doug placed his hands on the table and spread them over a foot apart. Then he raised both hands and formed a large circle.

Logan gulped. "Holy shit. What I wouldn't give."

Doug smiled. "I'd give you half if I could."

They broke into laughter.

Logan said, "I didn't see you in the showers."

"I don't shower. I bathe in the river."

"That's ice water! Are you crazy?"

Doug nodded. "That's what they say."

Logan looked into Doug's eyes again. "You know, you're a damn handsome man under that mop and mane. I can cut your hair. You're hiding under there."

Doug started to protest, but deep inside, a part of him craved the company of another soul. His heart spoke for him. "Yeah, I'd like that."

Logan's eyes lit up. "Really? Great!"

SHAVE AND A HAIRCUT,
TWO DICKS

At nightfall, Doug came back to camp. Logan left the campfire. He patted a leather portfolio. "Got my scissors and razor in here. Let's go to the changing room."

The cold Alpine air kept most men from showering at night, so they had the place to themselves.

Logan sat Doug down in front of a mirror. The older man was surprised at how much the face looking back at him resembled his one love, the heartbreaker Stew.

Logan put a bath towel around Doug's massive shoulders. It looked like a bib on him. The cherub went to work. Busy scissors snipped away the matted beard and shoulder-length hair. Doug's beauty emerged from under the curtain. His deep green eyes were no longer hidden. Logan was an excellent barber. He blew away the stray hairs and wiped Doug's face when he was done, leaving streaks of dirt on the white towel.

"Gosh, kid. I don't know who that is!"

Logan said, "See, I knew a handsome man was hiding under all that mess." He bent forward and kissed Doug's forehead.

Doug looked up at Logan. He closed his eyes and leaned forward. He didn't know if he was making a mistake and didn't care. Logan's lips met his, and they kissed. Logan put his hand in Doug's crotch and jumped.

"Oh my!"

Doug pulled away. "Don't ruin it. Don't start evil."

Logan ran his hand down Doug's leg to where his cock ended and his knee began. He squeezed the apple-sized head that was quickly becoming a grapefruit.

"Doug, I haven't had a shower in a week. Would you join me in case any bullies show up?"

Doug didn't know why he wanted to help this kid, but he did. Maybe it was that kiss; it was the first affection anyone had shown him in ten years.

"Yeah, let's go."

Both men blushed as they undressed. It was a conditioned response built up over the years of being shamed for being different between the legs. Doug couldn't imagine the shame of being small, but he knew the humiliation of being far too big. He felt a kinship. They unconsciously turned their backs to get completely naked.

When Doug turned around, Logan gasped. Doug saw the tiny penis on his new friend; he felt a mixture of pity and arousal. Something about that little dick made him horny. It stood at attention; the kid was clearly turned on by Doug's horse cock.

"M-may I touch it?"

Doug nodded. Logan stepped forward and caressed the monster with both hands, then lifted it to his lips and kissed it.

"I would love to try and take that."

Doug frowned. "Where would you take it?"

"In the butt."

Doug laughed. His first thought had been that Logan was literally going to take it, to steal it. He grew serious. "Logan, nobody in the history of my life has been able to take me."

Logan said, "I accept your challenge."

They showered in silence. Doug washed away the last of the stray hairs and cleaned his face with soap and hot water. Logan's tiny penis remained hard the whole time, not even as long or thick as Doug's pinky. The older man was at more than half-mast, which was rare. He soaped up his giant balls and cock, glad to rinse it away with hot water for once. He stood under the warm stream, looking at Logan's tiny package.

Logan soaped up his crack, vigorously scrubbing until it glowed pink.

Doug said, "Are you serious about what you said? I don't think it's physically possible."

Logan nodded. "I had a cruel stepfather who did... unnatural things to me. I can assure you it's physically possible."

Doug was astonished. "That's terrible!"

Logan shrugged. "I didn't want to like it, but I did. I came out here to Oregon to hide from him."

They toweled off, each admiring the other. Logan's eyes barely rose above Doug's waist. Doug stared at the boy's plump bottom, imagining what it would be like to feel the cheeks hugging his meat.

"Logan, how do we...?"

"We need privacy and Crisco. I'll stop in the cook house and meet you at your tent."

"My tent is half a mile away."

Logan said, "I know. I followed you back a couple of times."

RIGHT THERE

As Doug made the trek through the woods, he braced himself for disappointment. From puberty onwards, he had been too long and too thick to be with anyone. His dreams of a family and children evaporated with each woman who rejected him. Not one person had even attempted to have real sex with him. The bond he formed with Stew revealed his preference for men. Stew's disappearance left him desolate. He vowed to be alone for life. Logan was a black swan, appearing so randomly and making such bold claims. That was it. When Logan showed up, he would send him packing.

Doug stoked a fire to warm his bones. He poked it with a stick, waiting for Logan to come so he could send him away. He would never let someone break his heart again. Logan should have arrived. Doug's muscles rippled as he picked up a heavy log and threw it on the fire. He saw the kid approaching, but something was wrong. As he drew closer, Doug saw cuts and bruises on his face.

Logan smiled and waved. He limped over to the fire and sat down next to Doug.

"What happened?"

Logan shrugged. "When you're a little guy, you learn

to roll with the punches. I'm fine, but I need a minute to catch my breath."

Doug's protective instinct surged. "Who was it? I'll fucking kill them."

"You'd be out of a job. It was all of them. They took turns kicking and hitting me. It's okay; I'm used to it."

Doug took Logan into his arms. The boy curled up in the armpit, just like Doug had done with Stew ten years before. They sat like that, watching the fire paint the forest with dabs of light. They exchanged energy in that moment. All the safety Doug felt with Stew flowed to Logan, and all the love came rushing back. A spark of static electricity shocked them both.

"How bad are you hurt? Do you need to see the medic?"

Logan shook his head. "Just a few bruises and scratches. I'm fine."

Doug wondered if the little guy really was okay. He was.

"Look what I brought." He proudly held a can of Crisco. "I lubed up on the way over."

Doug was surprised when his cock snapped to attention at those words. The energy changed from tenderness to lust in an instant. Logan undid the straps of Doug's overalls and unbuttoned his Pendleton shirt.

"Stand up."

Logan worked Doug's overalls down until his trapped cock flew up, smacking the boy's face. Doug didn't wear underwear; he never could.

Doug sat down. Logan shucked his jeans and stepped close. They kissed. The boy grabbed the colossal cock and positioned it between his ass cheeks. He bent his knees, allowing gravity to push the tip into his hole. He breathed out.

This was as far as Doug ever got with anyone, so he was shocked when Logan bore down and pushed the head in. It was the size of a grapefruit and not as squishy. He looked at Logan, whose eyes fluttered and rolled back in his head.

"Oh fuck, that feels good!" The boy sat harder, forcing the head into his rectum. "Oh shit, right there. Oh, man."

There was still a foot of cock exposed to the open air, but Doug was happy. Nobody could do this. Logan bounced on the tip, letting another inch slip inside him. He scooped some Crisco and greased the shaft. Another inch, then all at once another two inches.

Logan said, "I don't think I can go any further yet."

Doug felt the pressure of the soft pink hole surrounding his cock. "This is farther than I've ever gone. It's okay if you want to stop."

Logan locked eyes with Doug. "I'm just resting. Don't worry."

A weight in Doug's chest lifted. He leaned back, intoxicated from the warm, wet pressure on his throbbing cock. Then Logan squatted down with a loud pop, and Doug felt his cock push through a hole deep inside the boy. Logan sat down until his round rump sat on Doug's lap. His rapid breathing worried Doug.

"Are you okay?"

Logan closed his eyes tightly and nodded. "Resting, again."

After a moment, Logan put his arms around Doug's neck. "Fuck me."

Doug was a virgin, but nature guided him. He leaned forward until Logan was on his back. The boy spread his knees to give him room to pivot his hips. The burly logger took slow short strokes. Logan reached up and kissed him. The complete connection between the two men fueled Doug's sexual drive. His strokes lengthened, and the pace increased. His cock passed in and out of the inner hole. The sound was like hands clapping.

"Oh god, fuck me harder!"

Doug didn't need convincing. He rammed his cock home repeatedly until the clapping sounded like applause. He noticed a lump in Logan's belly and realized it was him!

Logan's head thrashed from side to side. "Oh fuck! Keep going! Just like that!"

Doug's strokes grew longer and longer until his cock popped out, effortlessly flying back into the gaping hole he had created. The sight of Logan's stretched, yawning ass was the tipping point. He felt climax building. Logan pulled him to his lips, and they kissed passionately. Logan's breaths were fast and shallow. Without warning, his tiny cock spewed a hands-free load of cum. It kept coming in waves, like a woman's orgasm.

Doug reached the limit. "I'm gonna cum."

"Cum deep! Cum in me!"

Doug pushed forward, grinding his hips into Logan's perfect ass. He was as deep as he could go when he came. Logan panted. The lump in his belly subsided as Doug became soft. He stayed inside Logan until he got hard again.

Logan wriggled beneath him. "Do it again!"

And he did. Both men came quickly, even though it was the second round. When Doug got hard a third time, he thought Logan would evict him. But he begged for more. They fucked for hours that third time. After he left his third load in Logan's ass, he pulled out. A white torrent of cum cascaded out of the massive hole. Exhausted, the two men fell asleep in each other's arms. The campfire had long since burned out.

❉ 5 ❉

A WAGER

Doug woke up early and started the fire. He boiled coffee and river water in an enamel coffee pot. Logan limped out of the tent and sat gingerly on a log by the fire. It was Sunday, and they didn't have to work that day. Doug got out a frying pan and opened a tin of Spam. The smell of the sizzling meat mixed nicely with the taste of the coffee. The two men ate their breakfast in silence.

Logan put a hand on Doug's leg and rubbed his cock through his long johns. It jumped to attention immediately.

Doug said, "You want more?"

Logan nodded.

"Does it feel good?"

Logan smiled. "I've never had better."

Doug couldn't believe something could feel so good for both people at once. His cock gave as much pleasure as it got.

Logan knelt on all fours and applied Crisco to his ass. Doug was rock-hard. He got on his knees and scooted forward until he was near the hole. To his surprise, the boy's ass opened to swallow him up. He slipped in easily and slid so far he had to walk on his knees to keep pushing his massive meat inside Logan's beautiful ass. He rounded the corner and pushed past the inner hole with a pop. Scooting forward again, he was able to rest his hips against Logan's butt. Logan rocked forward and back, massaging Doug's fat cock with his insides.

"Oh shit, that feels good." Doug closed his eyes and grinned. He couldn't kiss Logan easily in this position, so he put his big rough hands on the boy's butt and rubbed it, squeezing the cheeks together to hug the base of his cock.

"Slap my ass."

Doug obliged.

"Harder!"

Doug smacked Logan's butt hard enough to raise a red welt. Logan rocked forward and back fast and deep. Doug thought he'd run out of cum the night before, but he felt a fresh batch boiling in his balls. Slapping with his left, he put his right hand on Logan's penis and rubbed gently. Logan shivered.

"Oh, that feels nice."

Logan used his left hand to hold Logan still while he fucked hard and fast. He rubbed harder and harder on Logan's cock until suddenly, his hand was wet and sticky with a massive load of cum. It was so hot he felt his balls boil over.

"Oh god! I'm cumming!" He held Logan against his pelvis and unleashed as much cum in one go as he had in three sessions the night before. He collapsed, sitting on his feet. Eight or nine inches came out, but he was still inside the boy and still hard.

Logan knelt forward until the huge cock popped out. Doug's cum poured out of the gaping hole. Doug was so hard his cock didn't even touch the ground. It jutted straight out. Logan saw the massive cock in the light of day.

"Fuck, you're big!"

Doug nodded. "Too big for you?"

"Never!" To prove his point, he put Doug's cock back inside and walked back all the way to Doug's hips. He rocked his ass back and forth in rapid jerks. He kept the rhythm steady for several minutes. Doug didn't have to do anything. Logan did all the work.

After another five minutes, Doug felt the churning in his loins that signaled orgasm. Just then, he saw Logan's little dick spit out another load of cum, and it was so hot he couldn't hold back.

"It's here!"

Logan picked up speed, rushing Doug to orgasm.

"Oh fuck. I'm cumming!" He jerked and thrashed as his balls emptied into Logan's ass. He squeezed out the last drops and sat back down on his feet. His cock grew soft. Logan's ass muscles pushed him out. The flaccid cock landed in the dirt.

Logan twirled around and kissed Doug. He felt another stirring. His cock slowly swelled. He pulled back.

"If we don't stop, we'll never get to bathe."

Logan raised an eyebrow. "In the river?"

Doug nodded.

"Oh, no. We're going to camp to take a hot shower." He stood. A trickle of cum escaped his ass and ran down one leg.

Doug blushed. "I don't want to shower."

Logan said, "We've got each other now. Who cares if they see what you have? Or what I don't have, for that matter."

Doug felt a deep-seated fear in his gut. The showers would be busy all morning. He had worked ten years to keep his big secret hidden, and he didn't want it getting out again. Men are envious and cruel. "I'm afraid."

Logan said, "You and me together, we're going to be fine. They all know about you; I heard it my first day."

Hearing that his isolation hadn't erased his reputation was painful. "Oh, shit. You aren't serious?"

"You're a legend in these parts. Bigfoot isn't as famous as Baloney. That's your nickname."

Doug shrugged. "Fuck. I guess it doesn't matter."

They got dressed and walked to camp.

All eyes turned towards the two men when they entered the bunkhouse for clean towels. There were whispers, snickers, and giggles. The other loggers were worse than a group of seventh-grade girls. Out in the woods, gossip is like television; it's the highest form of entertainment. Doug's ears turned red. But Logan remained cool. He nodded, smiled, and pretended to laugh. One of the loggers smacked him with a towel.

A furry logger named Sven said, "Pussy boy's back!"

Logan grinned. "I got more pussy than you'll ever get, Sven."

The room erupted in jeers. But they were directed at Sven, not Logan.

Sven gestured to Doug. "And Baloney's splittin' your pussy now?"

Logan held Doug back. "He's got more dick than all of you."

The room fell silent.

A Canadian named Pierre said, "Prove it."

Pierre's challenge was Doug's worst nightmare coming true. It was why he stayed away from the logging camp. But Logan was his little protector.

"I'll take bets. No two of you can beat him even if you add your length and width together."

Sven said, "What are we betting? Pierre, you care to join?"

Logan said, "You give your private bunk to Doug if he wins. And you stop calling him and me Baloney and Pussy Boy."

"Ha. Easy. And if we win?"

"We'll do your kitchen duty for the rest of the season."

"I got a big long Swedish dick. Pierre's a fat fucker, right Pierre?"

The Canadian nodded. "Thick as a brick."

Sven looked at Logan. "You're the whistlepunk. How much time we got?"

"We got at least an hour. You think you can get hard before that?"

Sven whipped out his soft blond cock. The pubic hairs looked almost transparent. It was small and wrinkled, but the wrinkles smoothed out and stretched as he stroked himself until he was fully hard. It was an impressive cock. "Measure it."

Logan pressed a ruler to the throbbing meat. It was 8 ½ inches long and 1 ½ inches wide at the base and the head's widest part. Another logger named Thor wrote it down on a notepad.

Pierre stepped up, lowering his jeans. His cock was buried in black pubic hairs. As he teased it out, it spilled out of his jeans. The length was average, but the width was massive. His cock head was tiny, maybe ¾ of an inch wide, but the middle of his shaft ballooned out like a football. The ruler said it was 2 ½ inches wide, and his length was 5¼ inches. Thor recorded and did the math.

Thor looked at Doug. "Unless you're bigger than 13 ¾ long and 4 inches wide, you lost." There were little laughs around the room. "Baloney's gonna lose."

Doug had never been in a situation where his size would work to his advantage. It made him feel confident. He unbuttoned his pants and let the soft elephant trunk flop out. The room gasped. It was longer soft than Sven's dick was hard. And broader, too. Doug concentrated, remembering his night of bliss with Logan. He looked down at Logan's perky ass and thought, "I've been there." It was incredibly arousing. He closed his eyes and stroked gently, teasing the monster to life. There were gasps and incredulous groans. He cupped his hand to hold up the heavy log of flesh. He felt his skin straining to hold the massive cock swelling underneath. The head turned red, like an apple. The flare of his cock head was enormous.

"Holy shit." Someone muttered it under their breath. It made Doug smile. "Look at that fucker. It's still growing!"

Logan placed the ruler at the base. The head extended beyond the end of the ruler, so he marked it with his finger and measured another three inches in length.

"Fifteen inches."

He turned the ruler crosswise across the corona. "Four and a half inches."

Sven turned beet red. "Fuck you, Pussy Boy."

The rest of the men in the room, including Pierre, shouted him down. "You can't call him that anymore!"

And now Doug had a private bunk in a tiny room with a locked door. For the first time, he felt proud of his deformed manhood. It was too big, but sometimes too big was a good thing. Pierre slapped him on the back. "Man, I really hoped you'd be doing the dishes tonight."

Doug smiled. "Look, if you ever need a hand, I'm gonna be around."

Sven shook his hand. "The rumors were nowhere near as big as the truth. I've never seen anything like it." His hand lingered, then brushed Doug's ass on the way down.

Doug tilted his head. "Did you just feel me up?"

Sven shrugged. "Your ass is your second best feature. I'd fuck you."

Logan approached with two clean towels. "Let's shower before the whistle."

Sven grinned. "Mind if I join you'se?"

6

FROM TOP TO BOTTOM

There were three shower heads open next to one another. The three men lathered up. Eyeballs popped, and a few dicks went up and down, but eventually, the shower room emptied, leaving only the three men. Sven's dick was throbbing and wouldn't go down. Logan was hard, too, not that anyone would notice. It took several minutes, but soon Doug was soaping his rock-hard monster, smiling at Sven.

"You ain't fucking me with that thing, man." Sven backed away, shaking his head.

Doug shrugged and turned to Logan. "You want this?" His cock was too heavy to stand on its own, and instead, it pointed toward Logan's little feet.

Logan held it, weighing the heavy cock. "We don't got much time, Doug."

"Then we'll have to be quick. Hey!" Doug turned, looking over his shoulder at Sven, whose finger was working its way into his ass.

The Swede knelt, burying his nose in Doug's muscular buttocks. His tongue invaded the tight hole. He was hung big, so he knew how to loosen up an asshole before trying anything serious.

Doug's knees buckled; he held the wall for support. The thought hadn't crossed his mind that someone would want to fuck him. He was so big it just always ended in a stalemate. This was something new. He wondered if getting fucked felt as good as being tongued. He doubted it.

Logan was still slippery inside from the after-breakfast fuck. With both hands behind his back, he held Doug's cock in front of his hole, backing up until it was lodged inside and needed no more support. He backed up further, jumping when Doug gave involuntary spasms brought on by Sven's tongue. Logan wiggled and pushed until Doug was well past his second hole. At last, he felt the front of Doug's things on his butt cheeks.

Sven stood and whispered in Doug's ear. "You ready for this?" He smacked Doug's ass with his big dick.

Doug put a hand on Logan's back to steady himself. "I don't know, Sven, I've never..."

Sven laughed. "Virgin? Fear not. I'm an expert ass fucker. I'll break you in gently."

Doug had his doubts, but before he could protest, Sven put the head at the hole and pushed until it popped in. Doug saw stars. It was more painful than he could have imagined. How did Logan take his whole cock?

To answer his question, Doug looked down, stunned that he was balls-deep inside the boy. Logan started to thrust to and fro, impaling himself on the giant meat. Doug felt so good that he almost missed it when Sven shoved another two inches inside him. A new wave of pain was underscored by a pleasurable pressure on his prostate. He felt his asshole pulse, giving Sven another opportunity to move forward. Each time Sven paused at the point of excruciating pain and instinctively knew when to press on as the pain diminished.

Doug liked the way Sven filled him up and felt ashamed about it. There was something primal about being used by another man. He thought of Logan, used by men for many years, and wondered if it felt different somehow. The boy reached behind and put a hand on Doug's leg, pulling him close. Doug held his waist and fucked in small strokes, careful not to dislodge Sven from his own butthole. Then he felt Sven pass the second hole. His legs buckled again, and he held on to Logan for support. It was a singular sensation, like the best part of taking a shit. Then he felt Sven's thighs on his own ass.

"Ready, buddy?"

Doug swallowed hard. "I guess so."

"Here goes." Sven pulled back seven inches or so and plunged back in. Doug expected pain but only got the pleasurable feeling of being penetrated. When the cock moved past the second hole, his own cock throbbed.

"Yes!" Logan felt the throbbing. He wanted more, and he got it. Sven kept pushing and pulling in long strokes, smashing through the rectum and up into Doug's colon. Doug's cock throbbed in time to the strokes. Logan leaked precum like a faucet.

Doug didn't have to do any work. Sven did all the pushing and pulling from behind him. Logan bounced forward and back in the front. They moved in rhythm as a single engine of male sex. Doug groaned. The pain had dissolved into pure pleasure.

Sven brushed his mustache against Doug's ear. "It's good. You like it, right?"

Doug nodded. He was too deep in ecstasy to lie. His shame took a backseat to pleasure.

Sven said, "Just wait." He went from 33 rpm to 78. His cockhead pounded mercilessly into Doug's shitter and past the inner hole. Doug saw stars again, but this time they were made out of diamonds. He swayed, causing Logan to shift from side to side as he engulfed Doug's long, wide dick.

Logan said, "Fuck, I'm gonna cum." His hands didn't

touch his penis as it shot several blasts of semen across the shower room.

Sven saw it fly. "Oh shit, kid. You're a fucking sperm cannon! Oh, damn, that's hot. Oh, fuck! Aargh!" He plunged all the way up Doug's ass and held it there, unleashing a torrent of cum.

Logan continued to ride the enormous dick. The blast of cum inside Doug's ass, coupled with Sven's shrinking cock withdrawing from his hole, was too much. His balls pulled up tight and spat a massive load deep inside Logan's stretched colon.

Sven smiled. "We got five minutes, boys."

They dressed quickly and rushed to the job site. Doug forgot and farted cum in his work pants. There was no time to clean up. He just hoped nobody would notice. Nobody did.

7

CIVILIZATION

Doug and Logan packed up the tent and moved into the logging camp. Doug's fear and isolation had vanished, and he grew proud of his nickname, "Baloney." They shared a room in the bunkhouse with Pierre and Sven. It was a loosely kept secret that Sven and Pierre were more than bunk mates. The four men were grateful for their arrangement as the days grew longer and hotter. Most nights, Doug fucked Logan, and Sven fucked Pierre. Once in a while, Pierre would fuck Logan while Sven fucked Doug. And a few nights, they went two rounds.

In June, the camp started talking about "Logger's Delight." It was a full day and night of vacation at midsummer. The whole logging camp would descend on Bend, Oregon, and get all the whoring and drinking out of their systems. The event was not restricted to just their logging camp. There were a half dozen camps near Bend, and they'd all come to town on the same day.

Doug and Logan thought they could bow out; they were wrong. The whole camp demanded they take part in the revelry. As the day drew closer, they relented.

The night before the big day, Doug asked Sven where they were staying.

Sven laughed. "At the whorehouse."

Doug said, "There are guys?"

Pierre overheard and guffawed. "We're not gonna pay to sleep with a boy."

Doug thought they were into men like he was. Was Logan going to find a woman too?

Logan put a reassuring hand on his arm. "You and I are special, Doug. We do this by choice, not circumstance."

Doug scratched his head. He'd never been with a woman and never wanted to be. He couldn't imagine what Sven or Pierre felt. Especially Pierre, who took Sven's big dick in his ass. He was confused and bewildered.

"Where are we gonna stay?"

Pierre calmed him down. "There's a hotel on Broadway. A few guys like you two always stay there. We'll show you."

That night Sven and Pierre bunked down early. "We gotta save it for the ladies."

Doug and Logan followed suit. Neither wanted to go to the Logger's Delight, but they had no choice. Doug had suggested they return to the tent, but the pressure from all the loggers was too much. They were going.

Early that morning, a large hay wagon parked in front of the mess house. The loggers piled in, some standing, others sitting. Logan sat in Doug's lap. The bumpy ride down the skidroad had an unintended effect. Logan's thick ass bounced on the logger's meat. Doug got hard. Logan put a surreptitious hand on Doug's leg and rubbed it.

Doug leaned forward. "Stop it, Logan. I'm showing." It was true. The giant head had swollen by his knee, making it look like he'd put both legs down one pant leg. Other loggers noticed. But Doug had earned their respect. To his surprise, nobody jeered or whistled.

Pierre smiled when he saw it. "Ready for the big day,

Baloney?" It wasn't mean; he was acknowledging Doug's size and affording him respect.

Doug said, "I don't think I'll ever be ready."

Pierre leaned forward and gave a conspiratorial wink. "You're gonna like the hotel. Trust me."

"What do you mean?"

Pierre shrugged. "I said, 'Trust me.' So trust me."

Doug leaned back and closed his eyes. He tried to think of something unsexy, like a giant tub of macaroni and cheese. His hard-on wouldn't go away. Even after they hit the highway, it was so full of potholes Logan kept bouncing. When the hay wagon stopped at the Bend River, the loggers jumped out shouting. Doug stood, his hard cock forming a third leg. The other loggers were so focused on pussy and booze they didn't even notice. The two lovers followed Sven and Pierre to Broadway, where they pointed out the Bend River Inn.

"That's where you guys go. Get a room early."

The Bend River Inn was an unassuming frontier hotel. The sign out front read, "Lodging - Room, Board, Bath House." The two men noticed loggers from other hay carts making a beeline for the hotel. They hurried up the steps.

The front desk clerk put on his reading glasses and smiled. "One room or two?"

Logan said, "Just one. Thanks."

The clerk said, "We have a Logger's Delight special. You get free breakfast tomorrow before you catch your ride back up."

They paid the ten dollars, collected their key, and headed upstairs to room 121. In the hallway, men wrapped in towels came and went from the shower room. The sound of strong, hot running water made Logan and Doug feel that sudden rush of joy one gets when re-entering civilization from the woods. A door opened at the end of the hall, and steam billowed out. A tall, lanky man in a soggy towel strolled towards them.

"Morning." He cocked his head and smiled.

"Morning."

The man's hips swayed as he turned the corner.

Logan looked at Doug. "I think we're in the right place."

Doug shook his head and laughed. "I'm still thinking the right place is back in the woods, but I'm gonna give this a chance."

Both men weren't ashamed to admit they wanted a good, strong, hot shower. The room had two small beds, two dressers, and one closet. They stripped. Logan wrapped the bath towel and hitched it. Doug had to hold the towel with one hand because his muscular waist was too wide.

"Let's steam first." Logan led the way to the dark steam room lit only by a muddy skylight. It smelled of sweat and cedar pine. They had the space to themselves, so Doug laid his towel flat on the bench and lay down. His giant cock rested between his legs. He cast an eye on Logan, who smiled back. Doug's pores opened up, letting a season's worth of dirt and grime ride away on a river of sweat. It felt good.

The showers beckoned. The two sweaty loggers hung their towels and strolled into the group showers. Half a dozen men were lathering and rinsing. When Doug entered, heads turned.

The air filled with expletives. "Holy shit!" "What the fuck?"

Like turkeys at feeding time, they started to crowd the hung logger.

Logan leaped between them. "Stop! Back off!"

Unlike turkeys, they didn't persist. The men backed off. Several had their hands on their cocks, jerking. The showers were communal, so there wasn't any way for Doug to get a private shower. He panicked, but Logan put a hand on the small of his back. "It'll be okay now. Just take your time."

Doug didn't like being the center of attention, but the sweat needed to be washed away, so he stayed. He and Logan lathered up, then turned and soaped each other's back.

A small, shy redhead named Sean approached Logan. "I'm sorry, you don't have to answer. How does it work with you two?"

Logan wrinkled his brow. "He's the dad, and I'm the mom."

The pint-sized guy shook his head. "That's not possible."

A bearded Italian man named Chesco interrupted. "I'll bet it's possible. Look at his ass." He pointed at Logan's butt, which had grey curtain flaps like a vagina. Doug had never noticed before. He felt guilty because it was his handiwork.

Chesco stroked a massive cock. It was dwarfed by Doug's, but it was a real whopper by any other standard. He rubbed it against Sean's freckled ass. Sean's soft cock was below average but nowhere near as tiny as Logan's.

Chesco said, "I'm the dad, and Sean here's the mom." The redhead blushed. The Italian continued. "We got a room with whisky, cigarettes, and one big bed, and we intend to use it. Care to join us?"

Doug shook his head. "I don't know; it's kind of weird." But Logan squeezed his hand.

He said, "Come on, Doug. I want to show off."

Doug didn't like the idea of performing for this couple, but Logan looked like a kid at Christmastime. He couldn't say no.

8

DINKEY AND DONKEY

Sean and Chesco's room was impressive. They booked the room where senators and congressmen might have stayed when visiting Bend. It had its own bathtub and toilet. Doug noted that it even had a peculiar drinking fountain in the bathroom with hot and cold water. It must be a foot washer.

Sean went into the bathroom with Logan. The water ran, and the toilet flushed a few times.

Chesco handed Doug a tub of Albolene.

"This is the best. You tried it yet?"

Doug shook his head.

The Italian said, "Let me help you."

He put a hand in the tub and took a generous heap of the gooey face cream. He applied it to Doug's rapidly swelling cock, which felt great. He doubled in length and width.

"Fucking hell!" Chesco jumped back, astonished at what his hand had done. "It's so big. I never seen anything like it."

Doug shrugged. His time in the logger camp had given him the confidence to accept compliments. Still, the attention was always unnerving.

The two smaller men emerged from the bathroom with smiles. Doug had no clue what they'd just done.

"All clean," Sean said.

Doug whispered in Logan's ear. "What were you doing in there?"

"They have a bidet. I washed my ass."

Doug put a finger on Logan's hole, and it was wet.

Chesco said, "I think you two are having me on. There's no way he can fuck you."

Logan grinned. "Wanna bet?"

"You're bluffing. Twenty dollars if Doug can fuck you all the way."

Logan got on all fours, his ass at waist level. "You're on." He pulled his ass cheeks apart, exposing his gaping hole.

Doug needed no prompting. He lifted his heavy log and placed it at the entrance to Logan's insides. In one confident thrust, he slipped the first three inches inside.

The Italian gave a startled gasp. "I said all the way, and that's not even..." He didn't finish his thought.

Doug pressed forward, stopping at the second hole to allow Logan to adapt. But his lover pushed back until the cock slipped into his colon.

Logan "All the way, Doug."

The massive logger thrust his hips forward until he was buried completely. His pubic hair brushed Logan's butt.

"Mamma mia!" The well-hung Italian jerked the base of his cock while his freckled friend sucked the tip. "Guys, I don't have twenty dollars."

Doug shrugged. "If he can take your whole cock in his mouth, we'll call it even."

Chesco looked at Sean, who nodded and closed his eyes. The dark-haired logger put his hands behind the freckled face and pulled. Sean gagged, took a deep breath, then relaxed, letting his friend squeeze past his tonsils. A large lump appeared in his throat that came to rest near the Adam's apple. Dark pubic hairs tickled the redhead's nose. He gagged and pulled back, gasping for air.

"We're even." Doug turned to concentrate on his lover. Buried deep inside, he switched positions so that he was seated on the edge of the bed with his lover facing outwards.

Chesco said, "I can see it inside him!" Sure enough, the outline of Doug's cock showed through the skinny boy's tummy. Logan dribbled clear precum on the floor as he rode the massive pole.

The door to the room was ajar. A face appeared in the crack, and a man entered. "Christ! That's impossible!" He whipped out his modest cock and began jerking. Several other men joined him until the room became crowded with gawking loggers.

Doug would have been horrified by all this attention a few months before. That wasn't the case anymore, thanks to Logan. The boy loved any kind of attention. It was contagious. Doug was turned on by the room full of men jacking off to his performance. He turned it up a notch and started fucking harder and harder.

Logan cried out. "Yes! Oh god, yes!"

That sent Doug into a frenzy. He pounded his lover harder than he ever had before. He picked Logan up and rotated him until they were eye to eye. He stood and carried him around the room, leaning him against walls and on side tables, fucking the living daylights out of him. Somebody handed him a whisky, and he took a big swig and kissed Logan, sharing his fiery drink.

A few more mouthfuls of whisky, and they were both drunk. Doug crashed onto the bed on top of Logan, fucking him missionary style for the big finish. As a batch of baby gravy simmered in his balls, he felt a warm rain. One by one, the men in the room were coming on his back. They surrounded the bed, chanting, "Come! Come! Come!"

Logan's eyes glazed over. He stared at Doug through a fog. "Come inside me. I want to feel you come."

The gravy boiled over. Fueled by the attention of a dozen men, Doug tensed. His glutes tightened, and his balls pulsed. He filled his lover with semen. Whisky-drunk and fully spent, he collapsed on top of Logan.

The next sensation Doug experienced was a firm hand applying cold Albolene to his ass crack. It was Chesco lubing him up. The men chanted, "Fuck him! Fuck him!" Chesco was bigger than Sven, and he wasn't sure he could take him. But he was drunk and didn't care enough to protest.

Chesco smiled. "You want it, don't you?"

Doug nodded. His ass cheeks parted, and a warm cock pushed its way inside. Doug was relaxed; he took the man with little resistance. As the Italian pressed forward, Doug grew hard again inside Logan.

Logan's eyes widened. "Oh, do it again, please!" He shifted underneath Doug to bring himself closer. Doug pushed up with his powerful arms to gain leverage for more powerful fucking. Chesco's extremely thick cock went deeper inside, surpassing Sven in depth and pressure. A new sensation overcame Doug. Chesco hit some spot in his colon that caused waves of pleasure to ripple through his body. The waves increased each time he hit that spot until his body spasmed. He closed his eyes and moaned.

When Doug opened his eyes, Sean was standing on the bed before him. His freckled cock was deceptively small when it was soft. Hard, it was a good six inches and just right for sucking. He inhaled the redhead, slurping and sucking. Knowing he could never get sucked, he put extra effort into pleasing Sean.

Chesco fucked Doug hard, pushing him deeper inside Logan. Sean held Doug's head and fucked his face. Doug was like a sex machine, pleasing three men at once. If you counted all the pleasure he gave the room full of spectators, he was a god of sexual energy. His huge cock was a battery that powered the engine of male sex.

Logan shuddered and released an involuntary ejaculation.

Doug thought he might pull out, but when he tried to, Logan grabbed his butt and pulled him close. "No, keep going."

Chesco was thickest about three inches from the base of his cock. That meant that each time he pushed in all the way, his cock squeezed Doug's prostate. At the same time, the tip would touch that strange spot in his colon that caused ripples of ecstasy. Each time Sean pushed past his tonsils, it caused both a gagging sensation and a more profound wave of pleasure. Logan's guts were throbbing around him, too. The engine was alive, fueled by sexual desire and Doug's gigantic cock.

All four men were lost in their private bliss but connected through Doug to one another. The subtle vibrations and violent spasms traversed the big logger and spread to all four men. In one giant shudder, Doug blasted Logan's guts as Sean came in his mouth, and Chesco blasted his innards. Logan came again with no hands.

Doug swallowed as much of Sean's cum as he could, but it overflowed, landing on Logan's belly below. The spectators contributed more cum to the tangled foursome of men on the bed. When Chesco withdrew, Doug blew a loud fart that sprayed his cum. He was still inside Logan, who wrapped his legs around his waist and said, "Don't pull out. Just stay."

"I gotta pee."

Logan gave a wicked grin. "Pee in me."

Doug was too drunk to protest. His bladder was full, and he let the warm piss fill his lover. That was too much pressure for Logan to withstand. He pulled away and ran to the bathroom. The whole room gasped when they saw Doug's entire cock for the first time since they came into the room.

"Jesus Christ!"

"Goddamn, that's huge!"

"Biggest I ever saw."

"Probably the biggest there is."

Doug gave a drunken wave to the audience. "Bet you can't take it."

There were no takers. Logan was indeed the only man who could take him. As he surveyed the faces, they couldn't hold a candle to his little treasure.

When Logan returned from the bathroom, he received a round of applause. After all, he was the one whose performance required the most talent. Logan bowed towards the men, then turned and bowed away, flexing his hole open to give them a glance down the cavern, which evoked more cheers and catcalls.

When he took Doug's hand, the crowd shouted, "Go, Dinkey! Go, Donkey!"

Logan ate up the attention. Doug was pleased that his coupling with Logan had earned them a great nickname. Dinkey and Donkey. Perfect. Logan said, "Come on, guys, it's Logger's Delight! Let's go paint the town red."

9

BEND OVER

Doug pulled on his jeans and buttoned his Pendleton. He was just drunk enough to give in and agree to an afternoon in the bars and saloons on Broadway. The streets overflowed with drunken revelers from all four logging camps. Fistfights broke out over girls. The weak-spirited loggers bent over in the road and vomited. To Doug, it looked as though the world were ending. He couldn't hide the prize in his pants; men and women alike made grabs for it as though he were just an object. He wasn't enjoying the bacchanalia.

"Can we just maybe walk along the river?"

Logan nodded. The two separated from the crowd and walked west toward the Deschutes River. The riverbank was overgrown with summer wildflowers. Bees gathered pollen while hummingbirds sucked nectar. It was the diametric opposite of Broadway. As they followed the river, they talked about the future.

"What are you doing this winter, Logan?"

"I can't go back home; my folks won't have me. Maybe I'll find a place in Portland."

Doug smiled. "I know a boarding house in Portland, and I stay there every winter; it's clean and cheap."

Logan grinned. "Like my men."

Doug felt a strange attraction toward Logan. His heart had been in solitary confinement for ten long years, and Logan had opened it up in a few short weeks. And now he was hoping the boy would stay by his side. He put a meaty paw on the kid's shoulder. "I'm serious. Will you stay with me this winter?"

Logan slowed to a stop. "Are you serious, Doug? I thought you were a loner."

Doug didn't want to get hurt; he backed down. "Oh, never mind. I was only testing you. Of course, I don't want company this winter. It's hard enough living with the three of you."

Logan interrupted him with a kiss on the lips.

Doug was confused. "What was that?"

"A kiss, dummy!"

"No, I mean, what did it mean?"

Logan rolled his eyes. "What do you want it to mean?"

Doug hesitated. He was going to get hurt. "I want it to mean that you love me."

The buzzing of bees and the chirping of sparrows punctuated the silence.

"Doug, I thought you already knew that I love you."

The big logger blushed. "I don't think you ever said it."

Logan shrugged. "Well, it's true. I love you. I love your body. I love your mind. I love your muscles, and of course, I love your big--"

It was Doug's turn to interrupt with a kiss. When they separated. Doug said, "In case you're wondering, that meant I love you, too."

In the distance, the sound of a plate glass window shattering broke through the sounds of the meadow.

"They're getting awfully rowdy."

Logan nodded. "Boys will be boys. I'm sure this town is used to it."

The two lovers stepped off the river trail into the

tall grass. They lay beside one another, lips touching, tongues exploring. It wasn't the hard, desperate kisses of sex. It was the sweet, tender kisses of romantic love. They gazed into each other's eyes and kissed some more.

Doug said, "We haven't had sex in our bed yet. Would you like that?"

Logan kissed Doug and said, "Yeah. I really would."

They brushed the mustard grass and foxtails off their clothes and returned to the Bend River Inn. Some wise-ass had painted a circle on top of the 'Ri' so it read "Bend Over Inn."

Doug shook his head. "This town is something else."

10

WE NEVER CLOSE

The passionate kissing continued in their room as they stripped off their clothes. Doug held Logan in his arms as they spooned. It wasn't long before the passion switched to lust. Logan reached behind and down, lifting Doug's massive appendage towards his bottom. He had to scoot a good foot away from him to get the head to line up with his ass. Doug held Logan's waist and pressed, sliding in smoothly on the two previous loads of cum and the leftover Albolene from the morning's adventure. Doug nearly cried tears of joy as he pressed his way further, not having to wait or back up. Logan was his completely. At last, the little spoon came to rest in the big spoon again. Doug rocked back and forth on his right side, sliding back and forth inside Logan.

They continued to fuck on their side for twenty minutes. When things heated up, Logan rotated so his knees were by his ears, and Logan was on top of him.

"You like that, Dinkey?"

Logan nodded.

"Can I cut loose?"

"Fuck me hard, Donkey."

Doug went into high gear. Like a locomotive leaving the station, he gathered speed, pummeling Logan's insides with his Paul Bunyan-sized cock. Logan's butt cheeks, normally twin globes, were stretched into a pair of parentheses. He began to tremble, then quiver, then shake. The continuous onslaught had pushed him into a full-body orgasm.

Logan's teeth chattered as he moaned. "Oh, Doug, I feel so full." Doug put a palm on the boy's stomach and felt his meat carving a path through his guts. The contact electrified the twitching skin, completing a circuit that Doug had never felt before. He was magnetically attached to Logan. And he began to quiver, too. Soon the two of them were in the throes of ecstasy. Each twitch and shake sent waves of pleasure through both of them, causing more energy to flow until the electricity sparked like a short circuit.

Doug shook his head violently, sprinkling sweat down onto Logan. A few droplets landed in his open mouth. He smiled at Doug. "You taste like big balls and chest hairs."

Doug laughed and planted his lips on his lover's. The kiss created even more sexual energy. Doug's muscular ass cheeks contracted and loosened over and over as he thrust into Logan. Logan put his hands on them and pulled in rhythm to the fucking. He reached under and cupped Doug's massive balls. They were churning. He squeezed gently, and Doug nearly collapsed.

"You're gonna make me come."

Logan smiled. "That's the idea." He squeezed harder. Doug snorted like a bull.

"I'm gonna fucking come."

"Do it. Come inside me."

Doug pounded furiously. He felt something wet near his navel. He saw, to his delight, that the fucking had caused Logan to ejaculate with no hands. It was the final straw.

"Ohhh!" Doug's balls lifted from Logan's hand, pulsating like a bee's stinger. Each pulse sent a steaming hot surge of cum up inside Logan. It lasted so long that he thought maybe he'd somehow crossed wires and was pissing again. But it was all hot, thick cum.

Doug started to pull out, but Logan grabbed his ass and held him in place. "Don't go. Don't take it out."

It was far too big to come out on its own, even when soft, so it stayed there all night while the town of Bend echoed with shrieks and yowls from the horny loggers outside their room. Every couple of hours, Logan would wake Doug, and they would fuck again. It went on all night. The following morning when Doug finally withdrew, an avalanche of cum spilled out of Logan's backside onto the bedspread. His ass cheeks didn't touch, and his hole gaped open.

Doug touched the cavernous opening, and it didn't snap shut like before. The two of them went to breakfast. Logan limped to the table and sat down gently. Many familiar faces smiled and winked at them. The pancakes were almost as good as sex.

EPILOGUE

Back in camp, Doug never tired of Sven's nightly assaults, which taught him how to be a better lover to Logan. While he was getting plowed, he would watch Pierre make love to Logan, learning even more moves. He wanted to be the best he could be for the boy.

Winter seemed a hundred years away, but the logger camp began to disband when the first snow fell. Pierre and Sven returned to their wives while Logan and Doug headed to Portland.

The boarding house was dreary, making the Bend Over Inn seem like a royal palace. Doug saw how unhappy Logan was, and that was when they discovered something surprising.

Doug had been working ten summers at logger camp in complete isolation. He'd barely spent twenty dollars a season on food. The rooming house in Portland was incredibly cheap. Doug had never kept a checkbook and was too embarrassed to ask at the bank. When he and Logan went in to see if they had enough to rent a house, they got the shock of their lives. Doug was wealthy. He had enough to buy a house and live comfortably for ten years!

The bank manager was all too happy to meet his

mysterious wealthy client and help him invest his savings wisely. He suggested income property.

Looking through the listings, Doug discovered that the Bend River Inn was for sale. The two lovers didn't have to think twice. They bought their favorite hotel and lived their days there, enjoying the company of many a traveler and, of course, hosting the "bachelors" at the Logger's Delight every year in August. Doug's cock became a legend. Tourists traveled to Bend just for the chance to see it. A lucky few got to touch it. The Bend River Inn guests always remarked that the two men running the joint, Dinkey and Donkey, had to be the happiest couple on Earth. They may have been right.

❧ II ❧
KWIKLUBE 5000

SNAKE

In Van Nuys, California, the car is king. On Friday nights, Van Nuys Boulevard gets so packed with cars that Los Angeles passed an ordinance forbidding more than one U-Turn in a six-hour period. That doesn't stop the classic car collectors, vatos, surfers, party girls, and queers from packing the street nightly in their automobiles. In L.A., that's how people go for a walk. Jack 'Snake' Elgin was a shrewd businessman. On a trip to Ogden, Utah, he saw a place where they change your oil in less than ten minutes. The driver can stay in the car because it never goes up on a hydraulic lift. There's a basement where the mechanics work through openings in the floor. Brilliant.

Snake opened the first quick change oil shop in the middle of Auto Row in Van Nuys. KwikLube 5000 promised a $9.00 oil change in ten minutes or less, or else it was free. He hired Fred Hiney and Paco Seja, two young men who recently graduated from Pierce College's Auto Repair vocational program. In the first week, the two mechanics serviced 800 cars with Snake's assistance. The second week, he hired an apprentice, Doug Cherry, a kid fresh out of Van Nuys High who graduated top of the class in Shop.

There were four slots for cars. The line was long but

moved at a steady pace. They averaged 1,000 vehicles a week. The shop opened at 7:30 am and closed when the line died out around 8:00 or 9:00 pm. Fred, Paco, and Doug were paid handsomely. Snake would be a millionaire in a year or two, so he didn't mind the high overhead labor costs. Nobody quit, so he lost no time training.

Snake got his nickname in the gym showers at Van Nuys High. He was a late bloomer. When puberty hit senior year, it hit him hard. His penis grew so fast, it hurt. By the middle of senior year, it hung halfway down his leg. Now, ten years later, it was nearly knee length and wrist thick. He met dozens of women who wanted to have a go, and he slept with a few. It always ended with them begging him to take it out. They would give him a handjob or just take their purse and leave. He considered his enormous tool a deformity. He couldn't have penetrative sex with any women. He might as well be dickless.

Before he opened KwikLube 5000, he was a mechanic at the Plymouth dealership on Van Nuys. A few years back, the DWP announced a planned water outage in his neighborhood. He noticed a public bath called Roman Holiday on Victory and Van Nuys. After work, Snake paid five dollars for admission, and his life was changed forever.

Snake was no queer. The all-male bath wasn't a place to wash up like he thought. Everyone received a towel and a key to a private changing room. They left their doors open. Most men were lying naked, ass up, face down on the bed. A few were sitting up, stroking themselves. One or two stood in the doorway, pulling on their cocks. Snake panicked. He needed a shower, so he closed the door to his room, got out of his coveralls, wrapped what he could of himself in the towel, and followed the sound of running water. As he passed men in the hall, they stared. His towel wasn't long enough to cover the bottom third of his cock. Most men followed him like the pied piper.

When he got to the shower, ten men piled in behind him, openly watching as he took off his towel. He heard gasps and even applause. As he showered, removing oil and grime from the shop, the men formed a half circle, masturbating. He was just soaping up his cock, but it might as well have been a Broadway show. His fear when he walked in changed to confidence as he lathered his massive tool. He had never experienced such open admiration. In school, it was taunts and jeers. In bed with women, it was screams for mercy.

"All right. Which one of you faggots is gonna let me stick my cock in them?" A few men walked away, but five or six remained. He took the prettiest queer by the hand and led him back to his room. This young man was small and skinny, with no dick. He was more woman than man. The queen knelt and took the end of Snake's cock in his mouth. It didn't seem possible for such a small man to have a mouth that could take him. No woman had ever taken more than the tip. This guy had it halfway down his throat! After ten minutes of watching the little fag choke, he got bored. Perhaps the guy had ESP because right then, he took Snake's spit-slicked pole out of his mouth and put it in his rear. It was almost comical to see the little man struggling, his tiny penis sticking straight out and dripping. But like a magic trick, Snake's monster cock vanished up the queen's butthole. It turned a corner and kept going until Snake's balls hit the man's taint.

The queen did all the fucking at first. Snake stood back and let the girly-man hump himself. Snake had never come inside anyone; he was accustomed to jacking himself off. Having this person engulfing his meat so completely was a huge turn-on. He didn't care that his date had a dick. He was a hole that he could fuck, at long last. Snake grabbed the man by the waist and undulated his hips. Instead of crying for him to stop, the queen said, "Oh Jesus! Don't slow down. Harder!"

Snake needed no further invitation. He withdrew in long strokes and plunged back in, his hips pounding mercilessly against the little man's backside. For the first time, with a grunt, he shot his load up the man's butt. When he pulled out, his cock was coated in cum and even a little shit and blood.

"Clean it up, boy!"

The queen swallowed Snake's dirty dick all the way, scrubbing it clean with his tonsils. He stood and left the room with no goodbyes. Snake didn't have to worry about getting him off. It was perfect.

Since that fateful night, Snake became a regular patron of the baths in the Valley. He had an annual membership at American Continental Baths on Cahuenga, and he often drove to Toluca Lake to Glen's Baths. He even went to the seedy Serpent 8 Baths in Burbank. He rarely showered at home. He put his dick in three or four holes every night. There was a line at his changing room door. He sat on the dirty mattress, massive cock in hand, screening potential mates. He shook his head at the ugly ones and at the greedy young men who wanted a ride too soon after their last tryst. A nod was a ticket to paradise for pretty boys and talented size queens. Nobody knew his name, not even his nickname. He loved fucking with no strings. It kept him satisfied and straight.

HIRED HANDS

The success of his business took time away from sex. He had to stay later and wake up earlier. When he didn't get off, he got cranky.

Fred was the first to say something. "Sir, I think you're putting in too many hours. You need a rest."

Snake curled his lip. "I can't take any fucking time to rest, Fred!" The handsome mechanic stepped back. Snake didn't mean to snap. "Fred, you're right, sorry. But what can I do?"

"I mean, you could hire someone," Fred offered.

"You know, you're right. Would you like to be a manager?"

"No, sir. I'm happy working on cars. Maybe you just need a bookkeeper."

The kid had a good head on his shoulders. "Do you know any?"

"Paco's sister does bookkeeping for a lot of places around the Valley."

That week, he hired Catalina Seja to do his books three nights a week. It meant he could leave early from now on. She quickly tied up the books and made deposits, leaving Snake time to visit the Baths.

Fred had a motive for getting Snake out of the shop early. The three men were alone together on the nights

Catalina didn't come. Paco lived with his entire family in Pacoima, and Fred was still at his parent's house in Winnetka. Doug lived down the street, but his folks were always around. The men had grown very close during those crazy first months before they figured out ways to save time and improve service. When Doug, the apprentice, showed up, it increased efficiency by more than fifty percent. It also created an unusual chemistry for the men. Working side by side, they soon discovered they were more than just a good team. These three men were all keeping the same secret.

Paco Seja, Fred Hiney, and Doug Cherry were gay. Paco wanted to turn the shop into a glorious orgy. He wanted to stick his brown dipstick into both these boys' mouths and asses. They both wanted it, too.

The first night Snake left early, Paco turned down the lights. He lay face down on the basket-weave rope net that protected mechanics from falling through the slot. Doug and Fred were downstairs sweeping up when they heard a whistle. They looked at the slot overhead. An extremely thick seven-inch cock was poking through the ropes.

The two men climbed the steps so each could lick one side of the massive piece of meat. Paco felt two tongues on his tool and smiled. They took turns licking and sucking until they were rewarded with sticky white frosting on their faces and down their throats.

This became a nightly ritual when Catalina wasn't working. Eventually, Paco became bold and lay on the net while his sister worked in the office. He pretended to be adjusting something with a wrench, and she never noticed.

Oral sex wasn't good enough. One night when they closed down the place, Paco rolled onto his back and let the two men ride his thick, cruel cock. They used waterless hand cleanser for lubricant. It burned a little, but it made sitting on Paco easy. Doug went first. He had been fucked regularly by a running back at Van Nuys High. He thought it would make riding Paco a little easier, but it didn't. The running back had a short, skinny dick. This was Doug's first whopper. He faced Paco, his own short fat dick flopping on the Mexican's belly as he impaled himself. It took many slow steps forward, but Doug got the whole prize. Fred blew Doug while Paco thrust hard into the tight hole. They were all young, so just being naked around one another was halfway to orgasm. In a short time, Paco flooded Doug's ass with baby salsa. Doug's fatty blasted a load down Fred's gullet.

Now it was Fred's turn. Fred was not well-hung. He had been bottoming since he started having sex. He had no choice. His tiny dick didn't even come into contact with Paco's abdomen when he sat facing him. Paco liked little dicks. They made him feel powerful and dominant. Fred was short and thin, so Paco lifted and carried him downstairs. Doug kept a lookout on the ground floor above.

Paco dropped Fred hard onto a workbench. His cock remained firmly planted in Fred's hole. Fred put his skinny legs on Paco's shoulders, and they fucked. Paco had wanted Fred since they went through the vocational training together. He never knew Fred was joto until they worked side by side. In shop class and at KwikLube, Fred continually stole glances at the huge lump in Paco's coveralls. Paco was rock-hard for hours. He had to beat off in the restroom to prevent painful blue balls.

Now they were copulating in the basement of their work. Doug watched through the netting, touching himself through his pants from the excitement and energy these two gave to one another. Paco stripped off his coveralls, revealing his perfectly round ass and chiseled chest. Fred pinched his titties, but Paco slapped his hand away. "You'll make me come too soon!" Paco had just inseminated Doug upstairs, but he had a few more loads in him. He had to look away when Fred's tiny penis started to drip prostate juice from the pressure of the fat brown cock. It turned him on too much. Fred put his finger in the clear sticky stream and tasted it. He gave another fingerful to Paco, who lapped it up greedily. "I milked that out of him," he thought. It excited him, and his cock became even more engorged with blood.

The added thickness caused Fred to whimper. It really hurt now, Lube or no lube. It also felt blissful. He was happiest when a huge cock filled his rectum and even banged a little at the back. Paco was pumping hard, building towards climax.

Doug pulled his fat shorty out and pumped it. He stood looking down through the net at the action below; he didn't hear Snake enter.

Snake saw Doug whacking off. He heard noises from downstairs. Fred was shrieking, "Yes! Paco! Oh god! Make me a woman!"

Paco answered, "You're my little bitch now, huh?"

"Yes, I'm your puta!"

Snake remained quiet. He wanted to see what happened next. By shifting gently, he could stay out of view and see all the action downstairs, plus Doug and his short fat pud.

"Touch my tetas now."

Fred stroked the brown nipples. Paco threw his head back. "Ay, carajo! Si!" His hips slapped Doug's cheeks, making a series of ever-louder smacks.

"Paco, you're making me come!" Fred leaned back on his elbows. His little dick turned into a sprinkler of hands-free semen.

Nothing turned Paco on more than performing so well that the guy had an orgasm. No-hands was ten times hotter. He was a stud—Más macho.

"I'm gonna shoot, Federico!" He called Fred by his Spanish name as a term of endearment.

"Shoot inside me!"

Fred didn't need to ask because hot Mexican juice was already spewing into his fuckhole.

"Ahh! Shit!" Paco shot cups of come into Fred.

Upstairs, Doug bent in anticipation and fired off another round of milky sperm. It sprinkled through the netting and soaked his coworkers.

Snake ran his hands up and down his left pant leg. His huge cock was hardening.

Downstairs, Paco was eating his own semen out of Fred's asshole like he was licking frosting from a bowl.

Snake applauded.

❧ 3 ❧

FRED'S LESSON

Doug spun around, hiding his thick nakedness with both hands. The expression on his face was priceless.

Paco whispered to Fred to stay quiet.

"I can hear you two lovebirds. Get your asses up here!"

There wasn't time to get their clothes, so the two men stood naked beside bare-assed Doug. Snake took charge.

"I call this meeting to order. The agenda is what the fuck is going on."

The men weren't sure how to read the grin on Snake's face. He could be angry or amused.

Paco started. "Uh, Mr. Jack, we were..." he trailed off because there was no explanation.

"Fucking," Snake said.

Nods and silence. The second hand of the clock sounded like a hammer.

"Are you three gentlemen queers?"

Paco shook his head, but the other two nodded.

Snake continued. "I am not a queer, but I love fucking queers. I never told you my nickname, did I? Did I!"

"N-no, sir."

Jack Elgin gestured to his left pant leg. "It's Snake," he squeezed his cock for emphasis.

Doug's jaw dropped. Fred dribbled. Paco closed his eyes.

"I need to get off, men. What are we gonna do about it? Any of you size queens?"

Fred nodded.

"Good, I'll start with Fred. Doug, you're next. Paco, I'm saving the best for last."

Paco broke out in a sweat.

Fred followed Snake into the dark office and closed the door. Doug and Paco couldn't see anything. What they heard struck fear in their hearts.

"Holy fuck! Is that you? It's twice as big as anything I've ever—ow!"

"You're slippery, man. Is that Paco's cum?"

"Yeah, it...Shit! Ow fuck! Motherfuck!" Fred's fists pounded the desk.

"I'm going all the way."

"What? That's it. It doesn't— Oww! Where is that? Did you rip me open? Why does it feel so good?"

"Shhh. Lie back and enjoy it in silence."

For ten minutes, there were grunts and moans. Fred broke the silence. "Oh shit, oh shit, you're making me come!"

Paco made fists. That was his bitch in there. Fucking mayate.

"Take it, you little whore."

There was the sound a hose makes underwater. You could hear come being fired up Fred's ass and squirting out with fart noises.

"Clean it up!"

Fred made slurping and gagging noises.

A minute later, he stumbled out, drunk with come. He put his head on Paco's shoulder. The Mexican man pulled violently away. Jealousy is universal.

❈ 4 ❈
DOUG'S TURN

Doug walked into the office and shut the door. He gulped at the sight of Snake's massive piece of meat.

"Come in, Son. You aren't a virgin, are you?"

"No, sir. In fact, Paco just fucked me a half hour ago."

Snake smiled. "Good. You're all stretched out and lubed up with come. Another man's come in a queer's ass is the best lube. I'm an expert on lube."

Doug laughed nervously.

"Doug, you're in for a real treat. I have been fucking queers in the ass almost every night for five years. I can fuck the tightest hole. He gestured towards the door and mouthed, "Like Paco."

"If you have had a thick cock in your ass like Paco's, mine isn't much thicker, so it's really the length you're scared of. You follow me?"

Doug nodded.

"And I know a place to put it."

"It's true!" Fred offered from the other side of the door.

"You ready? Hop up here."

Snake was surprisingly gentle as he lifted Doug's legs and leaned them on his shoulders. To put his cockhead against his anus, the boss had to take two steps back. The huge head pressed against the young man's slick hole. Doug whimpered.

"Don't be afraid. Shhh." He put a finger to Doug's lips. With smooth pressure, he leaned in, stretching the boy's hole open as his helmet-shaped head passed the sphincter. With a quiet pop, the corona slipped by.

"That was the thickest part, Doug. The rest is easy."

"You are never going to get the whole thing in."

"You're in for a big surprise." Snake was pressed against the back of the rectum. Doug looked down and gasped at how much more cock was still showing. It made his own cock jump with excitement and fear. "You're at the end. There's no mo-oh-oh-ore."

Snake had turned the corner and found his way into the left colon. He was so gentle that Doug barely felt the pain. He was tingling. With a smile, Snake saw Doug's thick meat dripping with juice. He continued his slide. Doug's eyes rolled back, and he moaned.

"What are you doing to me?"

"I call it fucking." Snake rocked his hips, gathering momentum. His head slipped in and out of Doug's colon faster and faster. The young man's belly was so flat, Snake's cock head was visible through the skin.

"Am I hurting you?"

Doug shook his head.

"Can I go faster?"

He nodded.

Snake moved from panther-fast to rabbit-quick. Doug cried out. The fast fucking made his voice flutter like he was yelling into a desk fan.

Snake pounded hard. Doug opened his legs into a V to make it easier for the giant to penetrate him. Snake smacked his ass just to feel the boy's sphincter tighten involuntarily.

Doug had entered a parallel dimension where he could feel only pleasure. His head lolled, and drool came out of the corner of his mouth. Snake was heroin. Doug pounded the desk over and over. His short thick penis ran continuously with clear fluid expressed from his prostate. His boss grew more excited watching the waterworks.

"Oh fuck, Doug, you're coming like a woman."

Doug snapped out of his reverie and looked. His penis was drooling seminal fluid in a puddle that filled his navel and overflowed. Doug saw the monster cockhead sliding under his skin. He and Snake locked eyes. Doug leaned forward, expecting a kiss. Snake snarled, "I ain't no queer."

Doug pointed to his dick. "But, sir, I'm a woman." He brought his lips to the man's hairy chest and suckled a nipple. Snake lost control. He grabbed Doug and kissed him passionately. It was his first kiss with a man, and it was way too good. He didn't want to like it, but he was more turned on than ever. Doug played with Snake's nipples. Now it was Snake's turn to moan.

"Fuck my pussy, Daddy."

Snake didn't like the young, thin, hairless man as a woman. It wasn't exciting. He liked having his long fat cock in a man's asshole.

"I'm fucking your ass, boy. Drop the pussy shit." Then he kissed him again. And again. Doug pinched hard on Snake's nipples. Snake howled.

"Here it comes, boy! Are you ready to take my load?"

"Yes, sir. I want it, Daddy. I want you to fill my hole."

And Snake did. He ground his lips and his hips into the boy as he unleashed a full load of come into the apprentice's hole. Hot semen splashed and raged like a river. Snake couldn't stop kissing the boy. He was lost in passion. This never happened at the Baths. He stayed thick and hard inside the boy as the kiss continued. They explored each other's tongues.

Doug smiled, pleased that he made his boss stay hard. The young man wiggled his ass, and Snake fired up his hips and humped him again. Doug twisted Snake's nipples and bit his lips. It made Snake crazy. He humped the boy hard until he orgasmed again. This time, he grew soft. As Snake slipped out, Doug jerked himself hard. As rivulets of sperm trickled from his ass, he shot a big spunky load on Snake's chest.

PACO'S TRAINING

Doug limped out of the office with a huge smile. He motioned to Paco.

"I ain't going."

"Paco! Get your ass in here!" The boss gave the orders.

Doug and Fred reassured him. "He's an expert. He'll open up a whole new world to you."

"I ain't like that!"

Paco shut the door behind him. Snake glared with folded arms. His gargantuan soft cock hung near his knees.

"Paco, I think the orgy was your idea."

"Nah, it was all of us. But I ain't a fag like them."

"No, you're not queer. Neither am I."

"So why you gonna fuck me, man?"

"Paco, let's make a deal. If you let me fuck you, then you can fuck me."

Paco's eyes lit up. He liked fucking guys because he exerted his masculinity over them. Fucking the boss with his colossal dick, that was a big win. Paco wasn't a virgin, despite his stated policy. He had some cousins who used him last summer. He secretly liked it. But they were tiny compared to Jack 'Snake' Elgin.

"Okay, boss man. Fuck me first."

Paco's ass was white and perfectly round. His tan line made it pop. At its heart was a tight pink hole. Snake buried his nose in the crack and licked the puckered flesh until it relaxed and let him in. He used his tongue to stretch and lubricate the inside. He pushed saliva into the rectum. As he ate Paco's ass, he grew hard once again. Paco recited Hail Mary in Spanish to keep his fear at bay. "Santa Maria, llena de gracia..."

Snake took a tub of Vaseline from the desk drawer and scooped a handful. He smeared it on Paco's hole and rubbed it liberally on his now swollen cock.

Despite his better judgment, Paco took a peek at Snake's huge hard tool. It was so much longer and thicker than when he walked in. He trembled.

"Hey, hey, hey, Paco. I have fucked dozens of first-timers. I know how to do it. You will feel far more pleasure than pain."

"I ain't no faggot."

"No, I understand. Me neither. We just like sex so much, we'll do it with men, too."

"Yeah, okay. Hurry up before I change my mind." Paco drew his knees to his ears and stretched his greasy hole. Snake needed no further invitation. He wanted to teach his technique to the mechanic for selfish reasons.

"Paco, I'll bet you start off your fucks like this." Snake crammed his whole head in. Paco screamed in pain. Snake pulled out. "It hurts, right?"

Paco nodded.

"You need to be extremely patient when you fuck an ass. It needs time to adapt."

Snake placed his well-lubed cockhead at the anus. He leaned gently, allowing the tip to stretch Paco. He waited there.

"It feels good, right?"

Paco nodded.

"This might hurt for a few seconds." Snake pushed the whole head except the corona into the boy.

"Ay! Pinche verga!" Paco relaxed, and the pain went away. He nodded.

Snake moved the corona quickly past the sphincter.

"Fuck!" As Paco recovered from the burst of pain, Snake slid slowly to the back of the rectum and rested there.

"You good?"

Paco gave a thumbs up. Snake pulled back a few inches and slid back in hard, bumping the rear wall. Paco jumped.

"It hurts, right?"

"Yeah."

"I'll bet you bang hard here. Am I right?"

Paco nodded.

How much better does this feel?" Snake bumped gently and repeatedly into the rear of the rectum, sliding just far enough out to ensure his corona slid back and forth over the prostate. With a grin, he saw Paco leak clear fluid.

"Oh shit, Mr. Jack—"

"Snake."

"Snake, please keep doing that. Ohhh fuuuck. It feels so fucking good."

Outside, the cruising on Van Nuys Boulevard was peaking. Car horns blared, sirens wailed. But here, inside the office of KwikLube 5000, Paco was being shown the path to heaven.

Snake indulged Paco's request, making him leak a puddle of pre-come. He scooped some up and fed it to the Mexican macho man. Paco stroked his long, fat cock until it got very hard.

"Paco, this feels good, but I'm going to show you something that makes us both feel great. First, take a look."

Paco looked at the many inches of exposed cock that wouldn't fit inside him.

"It's cold, and it wants to be warm."

"Too bad, man. Where can it go?"

"Here." Snake lifted Paco's left flank and angled his way past the rectum into the colon. Paco's eyes bulged. There was intense pain when the corona stretched past, but then it felt good.

"This next bit will be painful for maybe 30 seconds, but I promise you it will feel good after."

"Do it, Snake. Please."

Snake moved his corona back and forth through the inner rectum like a well-oiled piston.

"Fuck! Oh fuck! Pinche verga de mierda!" Tears leaked out of Pablo's eyes. But in less than a minute, his whole demeanor changed. He wiggled and shook. He sucked on his index finger. His cock stood at attention, saluting the boss.

"You're ready for the full show."

And Snake went into overdrive, fucking the hell out of Paco. His hips pounded into the man's butt cheeks. They were so round, he couldn't go all the way. Paco lifted his hips and spread his cheeks. "Fuck me, papa."

Paco's ass was beautiful. Spread open and stuffed full, it was exquisite. Just looking at his own huge cock disappearing into that big beautiful ass made Snake get harder. Paco felt the man grow inside him.

"Oh, boss, you're so fucking huge. I never been fucked like this."

Snake smiled at Paco's inadvertent confession. This wasn't his first fuck. He decided he could get a little rough. He was right. He slapped Paco's big gorgeous butt cheeks. When Paco groaned, he slapped with all his might. Paco squealed with delight. Snake pounded into the man hard enough to make a bump pop out on his belly. Paco put his hand there and swatted the huge cock head sliding under his belly fat. With his other hand, he jacked his big fat cock. It was an impressive piece of meat when not compared to the monster inside him.

Snake usually only fucked girly men with little penises. Seeing a huge cock made him feel queer. But since his kiss with Doug, he felt it was time to give up and just admit that he was queer. With the newfound freedom of thought, he found Paco's cock incredibly sexy. He couldn't wait for the well-hung mechanic to fuck him. He wished his huge cock were merely big like Paco's, not the ridiculous monster that scared women and attracted far too many men.

Paco was proud. He could tell his fucked up cousins that they were too small. He took a cock as long as a chorizo and twice as thick. He would push their ugly faces into the dirty couch and fuck them until they cried for mercy. Snake's lesson made him realize how rough he had been with other guys. He wanted to go gently like him. But he could never reach this place, this heavenly place deep inside. Still, he would stop banging the walls now that he knew how much it hurt. It would feel a lot better for the guys he fucked.

Snake, overcome with passion and newfound queerness, did something new. He leaned forward and put two or three inches of Paco's dick in his mouth. Paco loved it. He wanted to make his boss feel as good as he felt. He bucked and wriggled to make Snake's dick get extra friction and vibration. Snake fucked with abandon and sucked the juice leaking from Paco's thick tool. It created an electrical circuit: mouth to dick to ass to cock to mouth. The energy flowed and catapulted the two men beyond the breaking point. Paco bucked furiously, fucking his cock in and out of his boss's mouth. Snake sucked and fucked his handsome employee.

"Oh fuck, Boss, I'm coming!" Paco's big brown balls gathered and released a gushing stream of cum into Snake's mouth. Snake swallowed as much as he could while the rest ran down Paco's big tool.

Paco lay back, enjoying the violation of his insides.

His cock flopped onto his belly. The sight of Paco's fat cock slapping his belly did it for Snake.

"Oh fuck, Paco, it's coming. I'm coming!"

Paco felt a hot spray in his colon. He got a sperm enema. Snake licked Paco's tumescent cock clean while he unloaded squirt after squirt of come deep in the man's belly. Paco moaned and sighed. Tears formed and ran down his temples. His boss grew soft. As he withdrew from Paco, the man felt like a thick rope was being pulled from deep inside. It got him hard.

❧ 6 ❧

PACO RETURNS THE FAVOR

Paco stood up, releasing a flood of sperm and Vaseline into Snake's cupped hand. Snake used it to lubricate his ass and Paco's cock.

Snake sat on the desk and lay back, but Paco shook his head.

The two naked men left the office to the brightly lit auto shop.

Paco instructed his boss to lie face down on the safety net. He sent Doug and Fred downstairs, where they pulled the man's giant cock through the ropes and licked it like an ice cream cone.

Up top, Paco kneeled over his boss. He reached into his own runny ass and scooped up some more Vaseline and cum. He rubbed it on his cock. Following his earlier instruction, Paco only put the tip in, stretching Snake apart. The shop owner wiggled with discomfort. Paco moved the rest of the head in but forgot to stop at the corona.

"Take it out!" Snake felt like someone had shot him in the ass. But Paco kept sliding, and by the time he reached the end, Snake was quiet. Paco was determined to find the door to heaven. He had an inch to play with, more if he spread Snake's cheeks. He parted the man's hairy cheeks. Dominating this furry man made him giddy with power. He poked and fished, then found the hole. He pushed in all the way. The hole opened and took the whole head, stopping at the wide corona.

"Ow! Ow! Paco, please, don't."

"This is gonna hurt." Paco jackhammered in and out of the inner hole. His head was thicker than Snake's, so it took over a minute before Snake's shouts dissolved into moans. It helped that the crew in the basement were sucking and licking the giant fire hose cock hanging through the ropes.

"You like that, Boss?"

"Oh god, Paco. It hurt so bad."

"You give up?"

"It doesn't hurt now. It feels intense."

"Good, right?"

"It's great. You're doing a good job."

Paco fucked the shit out of his boss. He lifted a leg to get in real close. He pulled his hair and slapped his ass harder than his dad hit him with a belt. Snake knew he had it coming.

"Fuck me, Paco. Harder!"

Snake wanted to make up for the years of one-way fucking. Paco was a thick punisher, and he got rough. Because he couldn't stay in the inner hole, Paco would hit the rectum wall hard during vigorous fucking if his aim wasn't precise. Each time he did, Snake cursed or cried or screamed. It made him rock hard.

Downstairs, Doug and Fred had a fantastic view of the action and a huge prize to play with. They jerked themselves, watching the show and licking their boss like a lollipop. Fred managed to put the head in his mouth and then slide it deep. He was rewarded with a satisfied moan from above.

Snake thought he couldn't come again, but he was mistaken. Fred's oral skills were drawing him towards yet another climax. Paco's painful pounding dissolved into a pleasant pumping. His hole had never been fucked. He understood at last why men loved it so much. The pressure on his prostate felt better than fucking ass. He felt like a woman, feeling the Mexican man filling him completely. His ass throbbed with extreme pleasure. It was an anal orgasm. He felt the walls of his anus turn into a vagina. He was a whore.

"Paco, fuck my pussy."

Paco laughed. He made his boss his bitch. He felt the flesh walls contract over and over against his powerful thick cock. It was true; men had pussies too. It flipped a switch, and with minimal warning, he fell over a precipice.

"Oh shit, Snake, I'm coming."

"Me too!"

And as Paco filled his boss with warm Mexican sperm, Snake shot his load below. Fred pulled back, and the humongous cock became a fire sprinkler, spattering Doug and Fred with endless loads of semen. They licked each other clean and cleaned Snake's long tool with their tongues.

Paco lay across Snake, breathing hard. His cock was still hard, poked just inside the inner hole. He kissed Snake's neck and whispered, "Who's my bitch?"

"I am."

"Who's gonna beg for my dick every night?"

"I am."

As the cars cruised past the KwikLube every night, no one could suspect the place saw more sex than a bathhouse. Snake and Paco were two studs who fucked the bottoms before they took turns fucking each other. The rope safety net wore thin and had to be replaced. It was worth every penny.

❧ III ❧
HOTSHOT

HUGH JAYNESS

I saw the ad in "Trucker's World" magazine at the Phillip's 66 truck stop outside Pittsburgh, PA. It read:

"Wanted: Hotshot Oilfield drivers. Must have own truck with 4-ton hauling capacity. Will assist with commercial driver's license. Contact Pittsburgh LEhigh-4-4367".

My stepfather died the previous spring. He left me his International Harvester heavy-duty C-series that carried up to 8,800 pounds. I had always thought I might make good use of it, and this ad seemed like a real concrete solution.

You might wonder what I was doing at a truck stop if I wasn't a trucker. The truth is, I liked the food. Okay, that's half of it. I also liked the scene in the hot showers. Long-haul truckers use the showers after sleeping in the lot. The lot is a hotbed of prostitution, narcotics, and vice. Sleeping in the truck stop parking lot is free. Breakfast is cheap. Showers are even cheaper, and they include a grubby threadbare towel and a small square of Ivory soap. The thriftiest truckers don't waste their money on a lot-lizard; they let me blow them. If I got lucky, they'd even fuck me. So that's the real reason I was at the truck stop. Now that I've confessed my vice, I'm hesitant to tell my name. But I'll tell you. My name is Hugh Jayness, and I'm a homosexual.

Hotshot trucking was a brand-new field. The shippers hired pickup trucks and trailers instead of big rigs. The turnaround time on a big rig could be a long while. The companies tended to wait until their trucks were at capacity before sending them out. A hotshot was smaller. They were ideal for jobs that required same-day or next-day turnaround. I'd often wondered who the truckers were driving their own pick-ups with a heavy load in tow. They were hotshots. And I wanted to be one of them. So, I called the number.

"Avalon Trucking, how may I direct your call?"

"Uh, yeah, I'm calling about the ad in Trucker's World."

"One moment."

A deep male voice came on the line. "Avalon, this is Mack."

"Hi, Mack, I'm calling about the ad. I have a 5-ton pickup."

"With a gooseneck hitch?"

I wasn't sure. "Is that the ball thingy on the bumper?"

"Yeah, but we need it mounted in the truck bed."

"I don't know about that."

"We can help with that. Can you come by for a quick interview?"

❦ 2 ❦

MACK

Avalon Trucking was in an industrial park on the floor of a smoggy valley. The red brick building appeared gray from where I parked. The receptionist looked just like she sounded: plump and dowdy with a kind smile.

"Hugh? Go on in. Mack's expecting you." She sized me up with elevator eyes. "He's definitely expecting you."

Behind an oversized mahogany desk sat a man the size of a gorilla but not quite as hairy. He chomped on an unlit cigar. He stood and extended a beefy paw across his desk.

"Hugh? Pleased to meet you. Sit. Sit."

I sat, but he remained standing. With his hands on his hips, he looked to be six feet tall and five feet wide. Thick fur sprouted from his collar. His green eyes were fixed on me. He licked his lips.

I'm not a big guy in any way. I went to the YMCA to keep in shape, but it was hard for me to put on muscle. I'm 5'6" and weigh 134 pounds. My dick is a little below average. Okay, a lot below average. I have a really big butt. When I was a 98-pound weakling in high school, the big kids used to beat the crap out of me. When the beatings started, I used to hate it. By the time I was in senior year, I'd discovered that all that attention was intoxicating. Then, I made an even more remarkable discovery: These guys beating me up were frustrated. They just wanted a blow job. Three bullies became regulars in the supply closet in the multi-purpose room. Sometimes, I had to blow all three at once when they crashed my schedule. It was hard work, but I loved it.

So, when I saw the way Mack stared at me, I recognized what was about to happen. I was excited because he looked like a great fuck. I was disappointed because I really wanted the job. I didn't think he'd give it to me if we fucked.

"Hugh, can you lock the door?" Mack removed his tie and unbuttoned his shirt, revealing a carpet of fur covering massive pectoral muscles and a round belly that had seen more than its fair share of French fries. He stood, revealing the motherlode. Below his belt was a tell-tale bulge that stretched down his right thigh. His piercing green eyes followed mine as I stared at the growing lump in his pants.

"Come here."

I knelt at his feet. I unbuckled his belt and opened his fly. Most guys pop out when I do that. Not Mack. His cock was trapped in his right pant leg. On top of that, his ass was solid muscle and bigger than mine. I struggled to get them to slide over and down. At last, they came down.

I gasped aloud when his cock finally came loose and smacked my chin. Even though it was plenty long, it was so thick it actually looked short. But when I put one hand around it, I saw five inches of flesh still exposed to the air.

"Get it good and wet, boy."

I opened wide and forced the meat to the back of my throat. It was too thick to get past my tonsils. Or so I thought. Mack held the back of my head and forced me down until I felt my throat swell with his fat cock. I pulled back hard and coughed out a ball of phlegm, catching it in my hand. I slicked up the fat cock and jerked him for a minute before he pushed my face back down on his club-like cock. This time my throat was prepared, and I went all the way, burying my nose in his dick whiskers.

"That's the way, son. Let me fuck your throat." He held my head and swiveled his hips, fucking my mouth like it was a woman. I tasted the salty drip that meant he was about to reward me with a mouthful of cum.

But then he bent and lifted me up, letting his fat cock fall out of my mouth and slap his thigh. Mack fumbled with my belt and tore at my fly, pulling my pants down roughly. He pushed me over the desk and ripped a hole in my underwear before kneeling. His tongue on my hole was a rare treat. It was an oversized tongue with strong muscles. He forced his way into my hole, and it actually hurt a little. There was no way I would be able to take his dick. I had been with some above-average truckers, but nobody was as hung as Mack.

He grunted like a truffle-crazed hog as he probed my ass, making it slick with spit. He stood, his cock waving in the air, and opened his top right desk drawer, extracting a miniature tub of Vaseline. He wiped it on my asshole and spread some on his cock.

"You ready for this?"

I wasn't. I nodded. I felt the fat head press between my chubby ass cheeks and knock on my back door. I pushed out, allowing my hole to open a bit. That was all he needed. In one swift shove, he put the whole giant head in my ass. I covered my mouth to keep from screaming. I wanted him to back out, but I needed him inside me. He knew his limitations. He wasn't a regular guy who could just push his way in and start fucking. He backed up a little, which stretched my hole a bit wider, so it felt like a relief when he pushed forward another inch. He kept pushing slowly until he reached the bottom.

"All good?"

"Yes, sir." My face said "no", but he couldn't see it.

He pulled back and thrust forward, bumping the end of my hole. He pressed harder, making me stretch. I felt an urge to pee but held it in.

Like a locomotive, he picked up speed slowly but surely until he was bludgeoning my guts with his fat meat club. My arms holding me up on the desk shook, and then my legs buckled. A warm wave of pleasure was making my muscles twitch uncontrollably. The constant pounding at the rear wall pressed against my bladder. I was going to pee.

"Mack, I don't know how to say this..."

He knew. He emptied his inbox and put it in front of me. I unleashed a small amount of piss; then another stream escaped with each slam against that wall. Soon, I was relieved to find there was no more pee. His inbox was half full.

Now my dick was leaking precum. Thin strings dripped into the inbox at first, and then I started gushing. Mack's fat cock was squeezing it out of me. When he saw that, he sped up.

I wanted to see my new boss, but I was facing the desk. I reached behind me and put a hand on his ass, pulling him towards me in time with his thrusts.

"Mmmm, yeah! You're gonna make me come, boy."

I rubbed his upper belly and found my way through the thick underbrush to his nipple. I squeezed.

"Fuuuck!" He grabbed my waist, pushed all the way in, and stopped. I felt my ass filling with warm cum. It turned me on so badly, I shot my own load into the inbox without even touching myself.

The boss buried his mustache in my hair and kissed my scalp. "Good boy. Oh, such a good boy."

I felt him pull back and heard a wet syrupy sound as his cum followed his cock out of my hole. Then I felt a cum-soaked handkerchief wiping my backside. I stood, pulling up my pants. I turned to face my impaler. He was struggling to get his semi-hard cock back into his pants.

"Oh, uh, you're hired. Leave your number with Dinah on the way out. You're on call 24 hours a day, seven days a week. When we call, you drive. I'll have our best man, Deckard, take you on a ride-along. Don't worry, it pays."

"Mack, sir, how much does this job pay anyway?"

"Oh, like a hundred bucks a run. You might get six runs a week during busy season or four runs during downtime."

Six hundred a week! My rent was only twenty-five a month at the boarding house. I was going to be rich!

❧ 3 ❧

DECKARD COX

The boarding house had a shared pay phone. I nearly missed Deckard's call early the next morning because I had to limp my way downstairs.

"Hello?"

"Shared phone? That won't work, my friend. Get your own place with your own phone."

"Deckard?"

"Yeah. Deckard Cox. I'm coming to pick you up."

I gave him my address and went downstairs to wait for him. He was pretty obvious. A giant pickup truck with an empty 40-foot trailer stopped. The window rolled down. It was still dark out, so I couldn't make out his face.

"Hugh Jayness?"

"Yep. Deckard?"

"Get in."

I hopped in and shook hands with Deckard. His hand was soft and warm, and my small hand disappeared in its folds. I looked into his brown eyes. I took in a sharp breath when I saw just how handsome he was. He had a short brown-red beard and a smile that could sell ice to an Eskimo. His auburn hair was cut short in a way that framed his Hollywood face. He wore baggy black coveralls with his name embroidered over the heart.

He was all business. "We're a little behind. Normally I would drop this trailer at the end of the day, but I was too damn tired last night."

"So that's not your trailer?"

He laughed. "No, you pick up a trailer pre-loaded, in most cases, and you get an extra ten if you drop it off at the hub on the way back."

"I don't get it. How did the trailer get there already?"

"We got short-haul hub-and-spoke drivers who drop the trailer the morning of the pickup. Gives them extra time to load it up before we get there."

"So, one guy brings the trailer, and we pick it up."

Deckard nodded. "And if we drop it back at the hub, we get ten dollars more."

We drove to Youngstown, Ohio, to drop off the trailer at the Avalon hub, then returned to Pennsylvania to get our load. It was a 40-foot trailer with three dozen oil pipes strapped on. When we pulled into the lot, they gave us some paperwork and pointed us to the trailer. I hopped out.

"What are you doing?"

"I'll hook it up."

"Do you know how?" Deckard grinned.

I blushed. Of course, I didn't know how. I got back in the truck and watched him fill out paperwork. He had a wedding ring that made clicking noises against the pen. He was a southpaw. In the early morning light, I could see light freckles on his nose and cheeks.

"Take a picture, it'll last longer."

I blushed. "Sorry."

He shrugged. "Like what you see?"

I glanced again at his wedding ring.

He winked. "I interviewed with Mack just like you. Don't worry."

I wondered if his interview had gone the same way mine did. Judging by Deckard's extreme masculinity, I doubted it.

"Come on, help me get the trailer hitched."

We worked on opposite sides of the truck and locked it in quickly. Our drop-off was a shale field in Pine Bank, in an area of southwest PA they call "Pennsyltucky" because of the locals' heavy southern accent. The countryside was a refreshing break from the city. I watched the rolling green hills fly by. Cows stood in their pastures, looking blissfully unaware of their impending doom.

When we pulled up to the shale field, a large woman in a guard's uniform greeted us.

"Hi hon, y'all got something for me?"

"Just some pipe, ma'am." Deckard could do a Southern accent with the best of them. She took the paperwork and shooed us onto the lot. When we pulled into the loading area, I hopped down.

"Where you going now?"

"Aren't we going to unload?"

"Hell no. That's not our job." Deckard jumped down and came around the truck to make sure I wasn't unstrapping.

I held my hands up. "First day. Sorry."

"Believe me, you're a heck of a lot smarter than the men I've trained. It's a relief, really." He patted my shoulder affectionately. "Let's go get some coffee."

Inside the temporary modular offices was a grubby kitchen with a pot of coffee that looked like it had boiled down to a teaspoon from a quart.

Deckard emptied it into the sink and started a fresh pot. When he bent to get a coffee filter, I thought maybe I'd seen wrong. It looked like he was smuggling a python in his coveralls. When he stood up, I lost sight of it. He saw me shake my head in disbelief.

"Did you see it?"

I shrugged. "Seen what?"

"My dick. I know that face, Hugh. It's like you seen a ghost."

"Well, did I?"

Deckard looked around the empty kitchen. "Yeah, you did." He unbuttoned his coveralls from the belly down, reached in, and pulled out the biggest dick in Pennsylvania.

I felt my knees shake. Just looking at it gave me a boner. Not that anyone would notice.

Deckard eyed me closely. He was trying to gauge my reaction. "Well, did you see a ghost?"

Instead of answering, I reached forward and held it at the root. I tried to lift it, but it was too thick and heavy. It would take two hands to lift it.

Deckard slapped my hand. "Look, but don't touch. I can't get hard on the job." He expertly tucked the mammoth back into his loose coveralls and buttoned up. "Your turn."

I blushed. "Wh-what? Nah. That's okay."

"No, it isn't. What you packing?"

I shrugged and dropped my jeans.

Deckard whistled. "Shoot. That's too bad."

I turned red, half with shame and half with anger. "What do you mean? I don't need it anyway."

"We're both shit out of luck for different reasons."

The coffee was ready. He poured me a foam cup. It tasted like an oil slick, but it did the job.

I said, "I don't see how you're out of luck. You must have a line of ladies out the door."

He poured himself a cup. "I ain't met a woman yet who would even try to do it with me."

"Aren't you married?"

He glanced at the ring. "This thing's just to keep people at arm's length. I met a few guys who were willing to try, but no dice."

"Not even a blow job?"

He laughed. "I'd break his jaw."

I had never thought a guy could be too big. I patted his shoulder and said, "You're right. We're both unlucky."

"Come on, they gotta be done unloading by now. Let's go." On the way out, he used a pay phone to call the office.

"We're in luck, Hugh. We got a 4 pm pickup in Wheeling." It was noon. We had to drop off the empty trailer in Ohio and then double back to West Virginia.

"Isn't that cutting it kinda close?"

"We're riding empty both ways. Don't worry. You'll get the hang of timing this stuff.

Sure enough, we made it to Youngstown in half the time it took us to drive to Pine Bank. The roads were mostly empty in this part of the world. Not like Pittsburgh rush hour. We dropped off the trailer and high-tailed the truck down to Wheeling. The pickup was down a three-mile dirt road.

It rained a little, just enough to turn the dirt into mud. Deckard groaned. "I fucking hate dirt roads."

The load was destined for central PA in Altoona. We hitched the trailer in the rain and started back down the dirt road. The trick to not getting stuck was to keep it in low gear, moving at a constant rate. Stepping on the brakes was deadly.

"What time do we have to get there?"

"Oh, we're sitting on this load overnight. The office is probably closed anyway." About 500 feet from the highway, Deckard started looking both ways back and forth. "If there's a car, we're gonna get stuck."

Sure enough, not 30 feet from the highway, we saw the headlights of a Nash Rambler barreling along. Deckard was forced to step on the brakes. He tried just to slow down, but he had to stop. He pounded the steering wheel. "Fuck!"

I said, "You got four-wheel drive?"

He nodded. "But that trailer don't."

After the car passed, Deckard reversed a few inches, then tried to rock forward. His wheels spun in the mud. He turned off the engine and tapped me. "Turn on that radio and see if you can get the news."

I switched on the radio and found a station giving traffic reports for the area. In a little while, it turned to the weather. No more rain forecasted for the rest of the week.

Wheeling's Business strip was a short walk down the highway. Deckard locked up, and we hiked the mile or so to the nearest diner. We were both starving. The food was typical West Virginia greasy spoon fare. I had liver and onions with grits and collard greens. Deckard had a burger and fries. He phoned the office to tell them what was up. His plan was to wait for the mud to dry and haul ass in the morning. We had to get to Altoona by 9 am.

"Mack says he'll pay for a tow truck. I'll call him to meet us here."

A crotchety old man drove the tow truck. He chastised Deckard for foolish driving. Deckard rolled his eyes. There wasn't anything we could have done, but it was no use arguing with the son of a bitch. The tow truck got all four wheels onto the highway, and we pulled out.

Deckard looked at me and smiled. "It's your choice. We can head to Pittsburgh, and I'll drop you at home. If you want the full experience, we can get a room at the Motel 6 outside Altoona."

I didn't hesitate. "Motel 6. It's nicer than my place, anyway."

"Wise choice. You'll get paid more that way, too."

I still had no idea how much I was earning. I decided not to ask and let it be a happy surprise.

They were out of doubles, so we got a King. Deckard got the first shower. He came out with a bath towel around his waist. The head of his dick hung down below. I felt myself get hard again. In the shower, I thought about that big dick and how impossible it would be to have sex with Deckard.

When I got out of the shower, I was still hard. My tiny boner poked through the towel. Deckard noticed. Then I saw something amazing. Deckard started getting hard. The head changed color and lifted from between his legs. The towel fell to the floor. I made a wet spot in my towel.

"Deckard?"

"Yeah?"

"Do you want to try with me?"

He folded his arms and flopped down on the bed, heaving a loud sigh. "I stopped trying. It's too humiliating."

That was just about the saddest thing I'd heard in my life. I rested my head on Deckard's shoulder. I traced little circles around his nipples. Each rotation made Deckard's cock swell and harden.

I held the head up with both hands and clamped on like a lamprey. I swirled my tongue in rhythm with the circles I traced around his nipples. It didn't take long for him to start leaking precum. He put a hand on the back of my head and gently rubbed my scalp. I stretched my mouth further, letting the first inch or two of his head into my mouth. My tongue was trapped underneath, but I managed to wiggle it a bit. I put my mouth on the side of the shaft and ran up and down the entire length, licking and sucking the sides. My salivary glands went into overdrive. Soon, his whole cock was wet. I put two hands around the shaft. My fingers didn't quite touch. Then I stroked up and down. The damp skin gave no resistance.

Deckard laid his head back and moaned softly. The saliva began to dry up.

Deckard motioned towards the shaving kit on the sink. "I got some Albolene in there."

I applied some and spit a few times. The combination made him extra slippery. I could still feel an ache where Mack had fucked me so hard the day before. Absent-mindedly, I smeared some of the grease on my hole. I made up my mind. I was going to ride that pony if it killed me.

Despite its immense size, Deckard's cock stood straight up from his waist. I stood on the bed, straddling his waist.

"What are you doing?"

"Changing our luck."

He protested, but I put the head at my hole and sat on it like a barstool. The first inch went in smoothly, then it stopped. I bore down and felt the flare of his head stretching my hole beyond its limit. It felt like he was splitting me in two, like wooden chopsticks just before they snap. I lifted off, drooled into my hand, and wiped the corona with the mixture of grease and spit. To our mutual surprise, I heard a loud snap as Deckard's head popped inside me.

"Holy shit! What did you do?"

I grinned. Now that I'd passed the widest part of the head, I got a few more inches inside me before I ran out of space inside. There was nowhere else for him to go, or so I thought. I straightened and bent my knees, feeling him moving up and down inside me. I looked down at his green eyes. He smiled.

I knew at that moment that I had gone farther than anyone else. I was proud of my ass. It had taken its fair share of dicks. This was several helpings of dick, but I was working with it.

I picked up the pace. When I adjusted my weight, I lost my footing and fell to one knee. The cock made a sharp noise deep inside me and just kept going. The pain was blinding. For a moment, I thought I was about to die, but then it felt great.

"Are you okay, Hugh?"

I nodded. "I think you're in my colon." I was able to keep sitting, watching in fascination as the cock pressed outward above my belly button. In a few moments, I was sitting in Deckard's lap, stuffed like a turkey. Astonished, he stared at my face, tears forming in his eyes. I leaned forward, closed my eyes, and kissed his lips. He kissed back, slipping me a little tongue. He rolled until he was on top of me. He humped in and out in small strokes, making my belly stretch. I put a hand on the lump and stroked it. Deckard shuddered with joy.

He picked up the pace of his fucking and lengthened the strokes. I shook and shivered.

"Are you okay?"

I nodded. "Harder."

He pounded hard. I passed out. When I came to, I looked up to see Deckard's eyes closed. He hadn't seen me lose consciousness. I shook harder. It was like how you lose control when you ejaculate, but it was in my gut, not my dick. My dick was drooling precum all over Deckard's stomach. I wrapped my arms around his waist and held him close. We kissed again, this time with no restraint. He kissed my neck and gently chewed on my ear. He whispered as he nibbled. "Thank you."

I smiled. I wondered if he had any idea how good it felt for me. Sure, there was pain, but it was nothing compared to the electric shocks of pleasure he gave me. He buried himself deep and held.

"Are you coming?"

He shook his head. "I just want to remember this feeling of being completely inside you."

His cock was stretching my stomach hard. I rubbed hard, enough to make him feel it. His eyes widened when he saw the lump his cock made. I rubbed harder, and he shook.

"You're gonna make me come."

I smiled. "That's okay, right?"

He nodded. I rubbed and rubbed until his hips bucked, and I felt a tidal flow deep in my guts. He collapsed on top of me. I looked down at my cock and saw that I had already come a few minutes earlier and didn't even realize it. We stayed together, his manhood lodged in my colon, until he softened. Slowly, I pushed the soft cock out. It wound its way through my entrails and plopped onto the bed. I could feel the ceiling fan blowing wind through the cavernous hole in my backside. The cum was lodged so deep inside me, it didn't flow out. I wrapped a leg around Deckard's waist. He stared into my eyes.

"Did I hurt you?"

I nodded. "It hurt sometimes. But not the whole time."

He pulled back and leaned on an elbow. "I'm sorry. I didn't want to hurt you. Oh no."

I laughed. "I'm glad we did it. I might even do it again if you'll let me."

The look on Deckard's face was priceless. "Really? You'd do it again?"

I nodded. "But it'll have to be every day, or my ass will close up."

4

WAKE UP

The following day, we woke up at six for the complimentary breakfast. We were less than ten miles from our drop-off, so we had time to kill. Back up in the room, Deckard kept stealing glances at me.

I put a hand on my hip. "You've got to do it soon, or it'll close up."

This time, I let him do all the work. I lay on my back and watched him push his way into my aching backside. The pain was bad, but nothing like the night before. After a few tries, we found the spot where he could go past the second hole into my gut. I pulled him close, wrapping my legs around his waist and squeezing him into me. The lump on my belly was enormous. Back and forth, he sawed his way into me. He put a big soft hand over my cock and rubbed it. I wriggled, and he lifted off. I grabbed his hand and put it back.

"Keep doing that, and I'll keep doing this." I put both hands on the spot where his cock stretched me and rubbed vigorously. I felt his knees wobble. He leaned in to kiss me. With our lips locked, he stood up and carried me around the motel room, resting me on the sink, then the table, before returning to lie in the bed again. We kept going, wanting the lovemaking to last forever. Finally, he cried out. "Fuck! I'm coming!" His hand rubbed my tiny penis furiously. I shot a load in his sticky fingers. That same warm river flowed somewhere in my colon. He pulled out quickly, spilling last night's cum out my ass along with the fresh deposit he'd just made. The bedspread was a mess. That's what maids are for, right?

I looked at the clock. It was 8:30 am.

To save time, we washed off the sex together in the shower and jumped into our old clothes, making a dash for the truck. It was 8:59 when we pulled up to the site in Altoona.

After unloading, we deadheaded the trailer back to the Wheeling hub for the extra ten bucks. We enjoyed the time together. It was easy to make him laugh. We drove down the muddy road to the drop-off. Deckard phoned Mack and got another pickup at 4 pm, this time in Cincinnati.

"I got time to drop you off, but I hope you don't mind. I told Mack you needed a few more days with me before you were ready to drive on your own."

"Let's go. I've never been to Cincinnati."

5

HOT SHOWER

The load was three giant barrel-shaped pieces of concrete. They weighed just under the limit. They had to be dropped off outside Cincinnati, Ohio. It was a long drive, which meant we would sit on the load overnight again.

"Home, truck stop, or motel?"

I didn't hesitate. "Truck stop."

"You sure? We have to sleep in the truck."

I wanted to hit the showers with my new friend. Something about the risk and the lack of privacy turned me on. "Don't you want to show off in the showers?"

Deckard looked taken aback. "I don't like strangers looking at it. Just friends."

I smiled. "That means we were friends by the time we got to Pine Bank."

Deckard blushed. "I think it was even before that. You're so damn cute."

It was my turn to blush. We drove in silence for a while. Deckard put my hand in his. It should have been perfect. Now that I'd been with him, I could hardly be satisfied with something smaller. I'd had so many men, and none of them could do what Deckard did. Except I couldn't blow him. He was too big to fit in my mouth.

My mind is my own worst enemy. Holding hands,

driving down the scenic West Virginia highway, I ought to have been as close to heaven as you can get. Instead, I created hell. I had to suck cock. Not the useless, partial blow job that I could manage with Deckard. I needed my throat filled. For that, I would need someone smaller. It could still be enormous by most standards. I was talented. But it couldn't be ridiculously thick like Mack or Deckard. It had to be within reason.

It was those thoughts that made me dig in my heels and insist on the truck stop. Poor Deckard had no clue how selfish I was.

Around 9:00 pm, we pulled into the Dixie Truckers Home outside Cincinnati. Deckard said, "This one's got the best pie."

It advertised hot showers and 24-hour breakfast. I had steak and eggs for dinner. The coconut cream pie was the best I'd tasted. It was time to wash up before crashing in the truck. I paid fifty cents for two towels, and we climbed the stairs to the showers. Deckard wrapped the towel around his waist before removing his coveralls. He wedged the head in the waistband and covered it with his hand. That kept it from dangling below the towel line. The long, narrow, L-shaped room was like high school, with open showers lining opposite walls. There were at least a dozen men in there. Regular folks showered in the first room. There was no shower attendant, so once you turned the corner to the other half of the L, sex was right out in the open. A lot of men had their hands on their cocks. A couple of truckers were fucking against the far wall.

I turned to comment and saw the panic on Deckard's face.

"What's wrong?"

"You don't know what it's like to be big."

It was true. I didn't. "Don't rub it in."

"No, that's not what I meant. People can be awful."

I didn't believe him until I yanked his towel and

hung it on a hook. There was no hiding the monster between his legs. Then I realized what he meant.

Every head turned to stare. Like Night of the Living Dead, the shower zombies rushed him, wanting to touch it, feel it, kiss it, hold it. I pushed my way to the center of the mob and put my body in front of him, hiding the prize.

"Back off. He's mine!" I snarled at the zombies until they took a few steps back. Behind me, I felt Deckard's cock growing hard.

He leaned down and whispered. "Thanks. That was hot." I bent forward to make my ass more accessible. I'd already coated the inside with Albolene at our last bathroom break.

I spread my cheeks wide, stretching my already stretched hole and inviting him in. His cock was so long it rose between my legs and pushed on my dick. I realized I'd misjudged the distance, so I took a big step forward. I felt the head slide between my cheeks and rest at my hole. Deckard's soft hands held my waist to keep me from falling forward as he pushed his way in. Every jaw in the room hit the floor as I smoothly took inch after inch until my belly stretched and his hips landed on my butt.

The two men fucking in the corner stopped and stared. Everyone in this neck of the showers had rock-hard cocks, and they were jerking them. I studied the cocks until I saw a nice big one. It wasn't too thick but long enough to push past my tonsils. I motioned the man over. He leaped at the chance to be a part of our incredible union. I put the head on my tongue and slowly swallowed until it hit the tonsils. I grabbed his waist and pushed the head down my throat until his pubic hair tickled my nose.

Deckard fucked feverishly, in a hurry, likely afraid the zombies would try again. But I kept them at bay, even punching the pushiest ones to keep them from pawing my man. The sight of the huge cock stretching my belly was a powerful aphrodisiac. It wasn't but two minutes before I saw a white stream shoot skyward, landing on the back of my neck. Soon the room was like a cum sprinkler. Even the guy I was sucking couldn't hold back. I tasted salt, then sweet, then my throat filled with cum.

I had no choice but to swallow it all; he was too far down my esophagus. After I swallowed, he softened and withdrew. His long cock landed with a soft smack on his upper thigh. He faded back into the crowd of men, who were still jerking their cocks, rock-hard.

My own cock was throbbing and leaking clear precum onto the shower floor. But nobody really paid attention to my insignificant dick. All eyes were on my belly, where the outline of Deckard's cock was performing Punch and Judy on my internal organs. It was then that Deckard grabbed me by the waist and lifted my legs off the floor. His strong arms rotated me to face him. Twisting with my bowels full of his cock felt so good that I started to tremble. My arms and legs shook. He pushed me against the shower wall and fucked me until his twisted cock straightened itself. His chest pressed against mine so that his cock was pressed hard between us, and mine rubbed against his belly.

"Oh shit! Oh shit!" Deckard's legs trembled. "I'm gonna come!"

Just hearing the words was enough to make my tiny penis explode. I shot a load of cum in the narrow gap between us. It hit Deckard in the chin.

"Oh, Hugh. Oh fuck. I'm coming!" He wasn't lying. My lower bowels filled with his cum. I could feel his big balls pulsing like a bee stinger as they flooded me with their seed. I think everyone else could see as well because the sprinklers of cum started again. I looked up and saw two or three loads dripping from Deckard's auburn hair. I was probably just as dirty. Good thing we were in the showers.

After our command performance, we turned the corner and took a legitimate shower with the regular folks. But even there, I had to scare away a few married men who suddenly wanted to touch a big dick. It took a lot of shampoo before our hair felt right.

6

THE TEXAN

In the truck that night, we talked about what happened.

"I'm sorry I made you go there, Deckard. I see now what you mean."

He laughed. "I'm glad you did. I finally felt safe. You can imagine what it would have been like if you hadn't protected me."

It was nice to hear those words. As a passive homosexual, I rarely see myself in a position to rescue anyone. But Deckard was so vulnerable and afraid it just came naturally to me.

I tested the waters. "Is it okay that I gave that guy a blow job?"

Deckard shrugged. "I was a little jealous, but then heck, I was all the way inside you."

I lied a little. "It hurts less when I have something to suck on."

Deckard kissed my forehead. "Then you can suck on whoever or whatever you want."

We fell asleep spooning on the truck bench.

I woke up to go pee in the middle of the night. I was careful not to wake Deckard, who looked like a big, handsome baby when he slept.

The toilet had five urinals. It was empty. I went to

the urinal closest to the far wall, where most guys my size go to pee in private. A shadow filled the doorway, and I heard cowboy boots click on the tile. A big Texan stepped up to the urinal right next to me. That was a signal. I turned and watched as he extracted his fat cock from his Wranglers. He grinned.

"Feels good." He leaned over and looked at my dick. "Oh, sorry, guy."

He shook off his dick but didn't put it away. I watched it throb and grow. It was fat enough that I wasn't sure I could suck it if he didn't help. He turned to me. "Much obliged."

I knelt and put the swelling flesh in my mouth. It was very thick, but I got it to the back of my throat with no teeth. It wasn't long enough to pass my tonsils, which was a relief. I get sore throats from the fatties.

The Texan held my head and fucked my mouth with total disregard for my comfort, which was just how I liked it. I gagged once or twice, and he slapped my face. "Take it, boy."

I played with my own penis, turned on by this rude cowboy.

The door to the restroom opened. I couldn't see past the Texan hunk, but I knew that sex in a truck stop toilet in the middle of the night was an accepted activity. Whoever it was didn't want to join in, I guessed, because they took a stall.

I reached up and tweaked the Texan's nipple. He groaned. I twisted it hard, and he whooped.

"Damn! Oh shit! I'm gonna cum."

I grabbed his fat ass and pushed him to the back of my throat. He let out a three-day load that overflowed onto the restroom floor. I swallowed the rest, satisfied with my midnight snack.

He zipped up, tipped his hat, and left the restroom.

The stall opened. Deckard emerged with a scowl.

"What was that?"

"I thought you said it was okay." I knew that wasn't what he said, but I played dumb.

"I said you could do it when I was fucking you."

"Oh, shit. I misunderstood."

Deckard said, "I'm gonna sleep in one of those concrete tubes. You can have the truck."

It was the first time in my life that I regretted having sex. I washed my hands and rushed out to the truck. I saw Deckard curled up in a concrete tube, looking uncomfortable.

"Deckard, I'm sorry. Please, come snuggle in the truck with me."

Deckard folded his arms and pouted. "You hurt me, Hugh."

I decided to stop playing the dumb card. "I get it. I wasn't thinking. Please forgive me."

Deckard was easygoing. My shitty apology was enough. "Okay. I wouldn't have been able to sleep in this piece of shit anyway." He crawled out. His coveralls were covered with cement dust. I brushed him off, and we went back to spooning in the truck.

7

A ROUGHNECK

At sunrise, we wandered into the diner and had breakfast. Despite having showered, our three-day-old clothes were smelling pretty ripe. I went to the market and bought us t-shirts. Mine read, "I live to truck at the Dixie Truck Stop." Deckard's shirt read, "My big rig got washed at the Dixie Truck Stop." I also bought a stick of Old Spice to mask any stray odors. At 7:00, we took off for the drop site. Cincinnati traffic was worse than Pittsburgh. It took us 45 minutes to get from the truck stop to the drop. While they unstrapped, I went into the shale field office to buy a Pepsi from the machine. While I searched for the vending machine, I saw a brick-shithouse oil worker getting a cup of coffee. He looked at me, nodded, and adjusted his crotch. That was the moment I realized I was no better than a junkie when he sees a needle full of dope. I was powerless over dick.

I nodded back and followed the roughneck down the hall into a single bathroom. He pushed me against the wall and kissed me. I liked kissing, but it felt wrong. I only wanted to kiss Deckard. But I'm not the one calling the shots when a 250-pound pile of pure muscle is in charge. He stripped to the waist. He had a washboard stomach and huge, meaty pecs. I sucked on one of the nipples like a nursing infant. He pushed my head down to his crotch. I knelt and undid his button-fly jeans. His dick was beautiful, veiny, and about six inches by five — just right for sucking. I held on to his massive glutes and pressed him into my mouth. Six inches is just long enough to pass the tonsils. It was the perfect dick for sucking, in my opinion. He wore a wedding ring. I felt the cold metal on my ears while he shoved his dick down my throat.

"Oh fuck, man. My wife's pregnant again, and she don't suck dick."

He was a talker. I'm a listener. It was a good combination.

"Your mouth feels so good. I hope you're ready; I haven't shot my load in weeks."

I realized the more he talked, the longer it would take and the more explaining I would have to do. I tried a shortcut that works with pretty boys like this one. I rubbed his ass cheeks, then put a finger on his asshole and waited.

Either he'd say something like, "Watch it, you're gonna lose a finger," or he'd say nothing.

This guy was a total chatterbox. "Yeah. Put it in me." I licked my index and middle finger and pressed both into his hole.

"Oh, fuck yeah. Oh, man." Within a minute, I had two fingers knuckles deep in his ass. It worked.

"Oh shit. Oh fuck. Oh shit. Yeah. Yeah." Without warning, he came in my throat. I guzzled it down.

He wanted to talk some more, but I ran out of there. It had been at least ten minutes. I ran to the truck, where they were unstrapping. Deckard looked at me. "Where's your Pepsi?"

I hadn't considered a good lie, but one came to me. "They had the kind of machine where you gotta leave the bottle, so I drank it down as fast as I could."

Deckard shrugged. He didn't suspect. When the

roughneck walked past me and nodded, I smiled politely.

"Who's that?" Deckard asked absently.

"He pointed me to the vending machine. Nice guy."

Deckard was oblivious to my lies.

8

A BIG MOVE

This time, when Deckard phoned, there was no job waiting. We just had to deadhead back to the Avalon hub in Morgantown and then head home. It was a five-hour drive through Ohio, West Virginia, and a National Forest. The radio played some mountain music that fit the scenery. It faded out in West Virginia, replaced by a hellfire and damnation preacher.

Deckard switched the radio off. "When I talked to Mack, he said this was it. I gotta let you go out on your own after today."

I felt a knot in my stomach and a lump in my throat. We'd only known each other for three days, but they were the best three days of my life.

He continued. "So, I started thinking. You can say no, of course, but I wondered if maybe you'd like to move to my place. It's a two-story house with lots of bedrooms. You could have your own bathroom, too."

I didn't have to think. "Yeah, heck yeah."

"That way, you don't have to get your own place with your own phone, right?"

I nodded and grinned big. The part of me that wanted to suck dick woke up and started yelling inside my head. I ignored it.

"That would be great, Deckard. I live in a flop house right now anyways."

Deckard nodded. "If you don't like it, it will give you time to save up for your own place."

"Oh, I'll pay rent."

Deckard winked. "I paid off the mortgage a few years ago. This job pays really well, you know? I don't need your rent. Save your money."

Fortune had shone down on me. It gave me a new house, complete with a horse-hung boyfriend and a great new job to go with it. I realized that my eyes were watering. I turned away, pretending to look out the window, and wiped away the tears. I'd had a run of bad luck. Mom died when I was still in high school. My stepfather got black lung and passed last year. I was old enough to care for myself but young enough to wish I had somebody looking out for me. And here he was.

It was late afternoon when we pulled into the lot in Morgantown. We unhitched the trailer and drove back towards Pittsburgh.

"You hungry?'"

I nodded. "I could eat."

We were fifty miles from Pittsburgh, and I was famished. We stopped at a roadside diner called Mabel's. It was easy to stop, park, and enjoy our meal without a deadline or a trailer behind us.

"I've been here before. The steak is right out of the pasture, and they have the best bear claw you ever ate."

We had sirloin steak and potatoes with gravy. It was the freshest steak I'd ever had. For dessert, we split a massive bear claw, fresh out of the oven, dripping with butter.

At sunset, we pulled up in front of my grubby boarding house. "I'm just gonna get a few things." I looked at Deckard. "I mean, sorry, do you need a day or two to get my room ready?"

He laughed. I was hoping you'd move in today.

What am I gonna do tonight without you?" He grabbed his right leg and shook his cock for emphasis. I felt my butthole twitch with excitement. I was ruined for any other man. Deckard probably thought he'd die a virgin before he met me. I was made for his fat dick.

I shook my head to clear it, then went up and gave my notice to the landlord. I put my things into a few shopping bags. I really didn't have all that much because I kept a storage space for a buck a month.

I threw the stuff in the back of my truck and followed Deckard to a quiet neighborhood with colonial-style houses and rolling green lawns. It wasn't the suburbs, exactly, but it wasn't downtown, either.

9

HOUSEWARMING

Deckard's house had a lonely smell. He'd left there three days ago as a confirmed bachelor and came back with a boyfriend. The smell would go away after I cooked him a good meal.

My room was upstairs in the back, with a view of downtown in the distance. I had my own bathroom and a balcony. Deckard came in and stood behind me, rubbing my shoulders.

"Nice view," I said.

He didn't say anything, just kissed my neck. I felt his manhood pressing up against my backside. My little demon in my head was doing his best to destroy the relationship before it could even begin. The rest of me wanted that dick bad. I dropped my jeans and stepped out of them, giving Deckard free rein to use me how he wanted. He knelt, and I felt his tongue on my tail. He swirled it around the gaping hole he'd made the night before, getting it wet. I felt grease on his hand as he worked his fingers into my hole. It was smooth and easy.

I had to see his cock again. He had it out, squeezing a tube of lubricant up and down the length before working it around to the underside with his hands. He slicked up the head and put it right on my hole.

In a repeat of his performance in the showers, he slipped easily inside me and made the long journey to the depths of my bowels. I saw the head protrude and then felt his hips touch my butt cheeks. In truth, it was painful. But I wanted him inside me more than I wanted not to hurt. That's what made it easy.

There was something about the pain of being stretched beyond your limit, stuffed full of cock, that made everything turn on. My muscles twitched, and my insides contracted, squeezing Deckard's pole in rhythmic pulses.

"Damn, Hugh. That feels good!"

I smiled. "I ain't doing a thing."

Deckard leaned back, lifting me off my feet. Gravity caused me to sit down even further, and the bulge in my belly looked huge. He walked around the room, his arms wrapped tight, fucking me from behind. I got glassy-eyed, staring at the head of his cock as it punched my gut from below. Every muscle in my body was twitching, squeezing, contorting. My little dick was a leaky faucet. He rotated me around so I could face him. I wrapped my arms around his neck and held myself by his powerful shoulders.

Deckard strutted out onto the balcony. I looked around, sure that the neighbors would see. His house was backed up against some woods, with nobody in sight, just the skyscrapers in the distance. We kissed like newlyweds. It was too much for me. My little dick was rubbing against his navel. It got his belly slick, and before I knew it, I shot a load skyward, soaking his chin and my hair.

"Whoa!" He was excited to see his fuck buddy shooting a load without touching himself. I could feel the excitement as he fucked me harder.

"Yeah! Yeah!" I whined like a toddler asking for chocolate. "Give it to me! Yeah!"

He gave it to me. His whole body shook when he

erupted. I thought he might drop me, but he held tight. He walked me into the bathroom, where he grabbed a towel, which he laid out on the bed before putting me on top. When he pulled out, I leaked his gravy all over the towel. It looked like someone had dropped a half cup of condensed milk.

I washed up in my private bathroom before joining him in his bed at the front of the house. We cuddled before I drifted into a deep, dreamless sleep.

GOOSENECK HITCH

The next thing I knew, Deckard was shaking me awake. He handed me the phone.

"Hey, kid, it's Mack. Look, I got a job for you today. I need you to come by the office so we can sign your temporary license and get your gooseneck mounted. Etcetera."

The last word hung in the air. I knew what he wanted. I didn't feel like I had much choice.

"He, uh, he wants to come in; I mean, he wants ME to come in."

Deckard laughed. "I got a run to Morgantown this morning."

I was confused. He wasn't jealous. "Are you going to say something to him?"

He shook his head. "It's part of the job. I let him fuck me so I get the better routes."

Did I hear that right? "You and Mack... he does it... in the butt with you?"

Deckard put some bacon on to fry. "Yeah, before I met you, I had no choice about this stuff. You wouldn't know, but a lot of guys like to overpower a man who's got a bigger dick. It's some kind of macho thing, I guess."

"Before you met me, you were passive?"

"I was a bottom, yeah. By circumstance, not by choice. Now that I met you, I'll only do it to keep my job."

I frowned. "You didn't like it?"

Deckard turned down the heat so the bacon would crisp just right. "You know, I did like it. It was nothing like what I do with you, Hugh. It feels good, but I wanted to fuck someone, anyone, my whole life. And now you're here."

"So, if a big burly roughneck gives you that look and follows you into the bathroom, and then he wants to fuck, you'd turn him down?"

Deckard thought about it as he stacked bacon on two plates and cracked some eggs in the bacon fat. He looked right at me. "That's up to you, buddy. Aren't we together?"

I was hungry, and the breakfast smelled great. I put a couple of slices of bread in the toaster. "When two guys are together, the rules are different. We don't have to act like a married couple if we don't want to. I mean, we can make up our own rules."

Deckard gently turned the eggs. "Huh. But I think jealousy is the same no matter who it is."

The toast popped up. "I guess you're right."

Deckard got butter from the fridge, and we ate a good greasy breakfast. I didn't need to determine the rules on the first day. I washed dishes, and Deckard left for his Morgantown gig.

I got to the office around 8:30. I signed the papers, and Mack walked out to my truck with me. "We're going a few miles over to the custom shop."

The shop was bustling. They were one of only a few places that installed flatbed goosenecks. There were twelve bays, and ten were occupied. When they saw Mack in my passenger seat, one of the mechanics waved us into the closest bay.

Mack got out and shook the mechanic's hand. He

was tall and lanky, with big, oily hands and a great smile. I nodded at him. He came over, hand extended. "Jason." When we shook, I caught him looking me over. It wasn't as obvious as the roughneck, but I knew when someone was cruising. Jason was either the head mechanic or the owner. Mack was a VIP at his place. Jason waved over a handsome Puerto Rican in tight coveralls.

"Paco, I need you to service this truck pronto. We need a gooseneck for a 40-foot trailer."

"Yes, sir! Right away." Paco saluted his boss and ran off to start the work. I sensed a familiarity between them that might be more than professional.

Mack turned to Jason. "The kid here's gotta be in Columbus by 4 pm. We're cutting it close."

Jason nodded. "Hey, Mack, no sweat. Paco's gonna fix it all up right. We'll be done before noon."

Mack shifted back and forth on his feet. "Great. Great. Hey Jason, can I use your office? I gotta make a few phone calls."

Jason grinned. "Yeah, go ahead. Don't lock the door. I might need to make a few calls myself."

Mack grabbed my wrist. "Come on, kid. Let's make some calls."

Mack closed the blinds and rubbed his crotch. I like giving head, but I really didn't want to blow Mack again. He was just too thick. I watched him take it out. It was almost as fat as Deckard's but half as long. I remembered how he'd pounded my guts so hard it made me piss. I wondered if he'd made Deckard piss himself. It was hard to picture.

Mack lifted his heavy log skyward, expecting me to kneel down and worship it like last time. I decided otherwise. I was still slippery inside from last night's roll in the hay with Deckard. I saw a bottle of Rose Milk lotion on the desk. I strode over and pumped a pile into my hands, rubbing it on Mack's dick. Without waiting, I bent forward and backed my ass onto his head. It felt smaller than I remembered. Good. This might be easier than last time.

"Don't you wanna blow me, kid?"

"Nah, you're all lubed up. Go on, put it in me."

Mack grabbed my waist, expecting a struggle, but he popped in easily. He pushed his way to the end and started humping me. I felt that painful force on my bladder. I lifted one leg, putting it on the desk, to get the right angle. And then I leaned back all the way, forcing him into my colon with a loud pop.

"Oh shit. Did I just rip a hole in you?"

I shook my head. I slid back and forth to help him get the idea, directing him past my bladder and into the second hole.

I felt proud. "You like that?"

Mack humped me furiously, occasionally banging into my bladder but not relentlessly pounding it. It wasn't as intense as Deckard, but it was a good fuck.

The door opened, and Jason came in, swiftly slamming it behind him. I was still bent forward. He stood in front of me and unzipped his mechanic's overalls. He pulled out a long pink cock. He put it in my mouth soft. I sucked until it swelled up like a kielbasa. It was the right size for fucking my throat, and that's what he did. He pushed past my tonsils, then swung his hips back and forth, holding my head still to grind all the way in. I was stuffed full at both ends, happier than a hog in shit.

Mack grunted praise for my skills. "Your ass is a miracle."

Jason said, "His mouth is pretty fuckin' amazing."

I could suck Jason all day, but Mack was starting to hurt. His fat head popped in and out of my second hole so fast that it felt like a rug burn. I reached behind me and twisted a nipple. It was a trip wire, short-circuiting his system, bringing him to orgasm faster. In less than a minute, he moaned and threw his head back.

"I'm coming. Fuck. I'm coming." And he came. He pulled out and shot the last of it on my back.

Jason's eyes widened. "Damn, Mack. You're fucking huge!"

I knelt in front of Jason and held his butt in my hands. I pushed him down my throat and held him there. My throat pulsed, causing Jason to throb. Just holding him there, the pulses and throbbing swelled to a crescendo. He grabbed my hair.

"Shit! Oh, fuck how did you do that? I'm gonna —"

He trailed off in bliss as he fed my gullet a steaming hot lunch of sperm. I had to breathe, so I pulled back and sucked air hard. Jason's cock fell out of my mouth. He tucked it back inside. Mack was still so blown away; he was just leaning against the desk with his dick out.

Jason laughed. "Put that monster away, Mack."

Mack snapped out of his daydream and zipped it away. "Hugh, what was that? How did you do that?"

Jason said, "Do what?"

He said, "He took me all the way. It's like he had a second hole."

Jason laughed. "I guess you're too thick to go there. I go there all the time." I figured it was with Paco. "Hugh, how did you fit that monster past your second hole?"

I shrugged. "Just talented, I guess."

❧ II ❧

A PICKUP SITE

At 12:15 pm, Paco finished mounting and welding the gooseneck to my truck bed. Columbus is more than three hours away. It was going to be a tight trip. To make matters worse, I had to haul the payload all the way to Bowling Green, Kentucky, another five hours southwest.

I wasn't going to have time to stop for lunch. Jason's cum would have to be my only meal until dinner. I had a road atlas and maps of Columbus and Bowling Green. I'd never been to Kentucky. I was excited about it.

Highway 70 is a busy road. I drove fast, but not enough to draw the attention of the Ohio Highway Patrol. Columbus was still 100 miles away at 2 pm. I had to study the map in the truck so I'd know what exit to take. I noticed a small notebook with a pen beside me on the seat. I crumpled the map of Columbus down to a manageable size and flipped the notebook open. The first page was in Deckard's writing.

"Good luck, little buddy. I'll be thinking of you. PS - Write down your turns and exits before you set out." There was a heart at the bottom of the page.

"Duly noted," I said to an imaginary Deckard.

I checked the time when Columbus was 40 miles away. It was 3 pm. I pulled into a busy rest area. I was fumbling with the map when a physically fit trucker tapped on his window.

"Need help with the map?"

"Nah, I'm good."

"You look good."

Shit. He had one hour to get at least 40 miles, maybe more. There was no time for whatever this fellow had in mind.

"Hotshot?"

I nodded. "Yeah, I gotta be somewhere in Columbus in an hour. Don't get me wrong. You look fucking great. I just don't have time."

The trucker grabbed his crotch. "You sure?"

I found the exit on the map just then. It was less than 20 miles.

"Make it quick."

I followed him to a massive semi with a mattress for a back seat. He lay back, letting his cock out of his jeans. It was small and soft. I put the whole thing in my mouth, and it swelled like a balloon until it was at least eight inches. Lucky man.

I took him in my throat and worked hard. I wriggled a finger into his crack, but he slapped my hand away. I tweaked a nipple, and he smacked my hand again. I was out of joy buzzers. I could feel the minutes tick by. At last, the guy grabbed my head, fucking my throat hard, feeding me his semen in giant spurts.

"Thanks, man. Cigarette?" He held up a pack of Lucky Strikes.

"No, gotta run." I checked my watch. It was 3:30. Shit!

I buttoned up as I ran back to my truck. I pulled out and hit some kind of bullshit rush-hour traffic three miles from my exit. I'd forgotten to write down the rest of the directions, so I fumbled again with the map. The address was on Blacklick Road in Etna. Exit 310 South, left on Blacklick. Thank God it was easy.

It was 3:58 when I pulled into the pickup site and backed my truck up to the trailer. They handed me a ton of paperwork, and I started to fill it out, but one of the guys said, "You gotta hitch by 4:00, or it's unpaid."

With 30 seconds left, I slammed the trailer into the gooseneck, tightened it, and hopped back in the truck. "Are we good?"

The guy said, "Yeah, I was just pulling your leg." Bastard.

I filled out the paperwork to the best of my ability and handed it back. He went over it with me, which he didn't have to do, and collected it back before sending me down the road to Bowling Green.

I pulled over to the side of the road and got my little notebook—70 West to the 71 South to Cincinnati and Louisville, then the 65 South to Bowling Green. Exit 234 North (or maybe West) to Cemetery Road, and look for the sign for Pipeways Shale and Steam.

I was hungry, but I needed to make good time so as to get south of Louisville and avoid rush-hour traffic in the morning. So, I stopped at an A&W for a cheese-burger and root beer. I ate on the road. It was dark when I reached Cincinnati.

12

THREE STOOGES

Driving through the bustling city with a 40-foot trailer hitched to my truck was no picnic. There was a ring road, but I missed it and had to go straight through the center of town. Cars honked any time I tried to change lanes. I understood. I'm sure I've honked at my fair share of trucks. But now I see why they do what they do. You have to startle a car, or they'll never let you over. I nearly exited twice, passing through the center of town. Drivers passed me, flipping the bird. Kids stuck their thumbs in their ears and blew raspberries. It was something I hadn't noticed as a passenger with Deckard. Then again, he had been driving this way for years, and this was my maiden voyage. To make matters worse, I was nodding to sleep.

On the outskirts of Cincinnati, I saw a truck motel. It had places to park a big rig or trailer and rooms to crash. I paid the five bucks for a room. All the rooms had single beds. My bed was neatly made. There was no dust on the windowsills, and the room smelled fresh. I had to be in Bowling Green by 9:00 am, so I phoned the front desk and asked for a 5:00 am wake-up call. The place had hall showers, which I soon discovered was a perfect setup.

I wrapped a towel around my waist and followed the

sound of running water and laughter to a shower room. They were individual showers with stalls, but the curtains had long since rotted off the shower rod.

Three friends were horsing around, throwing soap at each other, and talking pussy. There was a man in his thirties with black curly hair, another man in his thirties with blond hair, and a brown-haired young man with no body hair anywhere but his crotch. When I came in, the youngest one greeted me.

"Hey man, you like eating pussy, or fucking pussy?"

It wasn't the first time I'd been asked. I hung up my towel and pointed to my dick. "Eating."

The young guy looked crestfallen. "Oh, man, I'm sorry. I mean, damn."

I shrugged. A bar of soap went flying through the air and hit me in the head.

"Oh shit!" The blond grinned sheepishly. That was meant for Tucker."

"Man, fuck you, Grant!" Tucker, the youngster, grabbed the soap from my stall, not even aware he had brushed my crotch with his ear. He threw it hard and missed Grant, the blond, hitting the guy with curly black hair instead. This could get ugly, but they were laughing, and nobody seemed to care.

In these situations, I make it a rule to keep my eyes above the waist until I see someone else's eyes go south. Looking around the room, the three men didn't even glance at me. Tucker and Grant toweled off and went back to their rooms. The curly-haired fellow was lingering; I saw him look at my ass, so I looked at his crotch. Holy shit! When it rains, it pours. This guy was hung long and thick. He was longer than Mack and thicker than Jason. It bobbed up and down as he fiddled with the tiny shampoo bottles and miniature bars of soap.

He looked me up and down, grinning. "Name's Beau, but my friends call me Curly."

"Hugh."

The sound of the showers was deafening in the silence. Curly scratched his balls. I bent over to pick up my fallen bar of soap. Beau whistled. "Damn, you got a big ass. It's like my old lady's, only younger and tighter."

I pointed. "You fuck her with that thing?"

"She don't always walk right after, but yeah. What's your lady think of your situation down there?"

"I ain't got a lady." I did my best to imply what that meant. Curly wasn't the brightest bulb in the pack, but he got me. I toweled off, staring at his big, beautiful cock the whole time.

"I'm sharing the room with my son Tucker. He don't know about this stuff."

"I'm in room 108. Meet me there in ten." I returned to my room, took a dump, and wiped Albolene up in my hole. I left the door unlocked and lay on the bed with my knees bent, legs apart. There was a knock.

"Come in."

It was Tucker, Grant, and Curly. Tucker looked like a deer in headlights. Grant just looked hungry. Curly was rock-hard under his towel. He started to bark orders to his crew.

"Tucker, sit on his chest so he can suck you. Grant, you and me are going in together."

I was a little worried that I had no say in the matter. I was like an object to be used and hopefully discarded. I didn't want to think what would happen if they tied me up. They might have knives or guns or axes. I just had to trust them.

Tucker sat on my chest. He was a chip off the old block. His cock was already big, and it swelled up when I started licking the head. He was really inexperienced, of course, so I did my best to show him the way. I put the whole thing in my mouth as it lengthened and swelled to fill my mouth.

Meanwhile, Grant and Curly were debating who should go in first. They decided on Curly. He pushed my legs high and pulled me to the edge of the bed. This made Tucker rock forward, going into my throat.

Curly pushed in hard. His technique was to 'shove it all in before they complain.' I'm sure it lost him a lot of lovers. Luckily, I was well stretched from this morning with Mack. He reached the end and, to his surprise, kept going. "Damn! Did I poke a hole in you?"

It was hard for me to believe a man as big as Curly had never been past the second hole. "You're good, man."

"That's what my old lady says." He chuckled at his own joke. "Come on in, Grant, the water's fine." Curly held my ankles close to my ears and climbed onto the bed. Grant stepped forward. I had never looked at his dick, so I didn't know what was coming. Curly was already really thick. If Grant were the same, there wouldn't be room. I tried to see past Tucker and Curly, but it was no use. My mouth was full, so I couldn't even ask.

Grant poked the head in. It was a small head. I breathed a premature sigh of relief. The shaft was just as thick as Curly's. He pushed in next to his friend, letting his downward thrusts ease him in alongside. I thought my ass might split open. I whimpered a little.

Curly said, "He's crying. Should we stop?"

Grant said, "Nah! Fuck him!"

I got worried about who I'd let in my room. Sadists aren't usually the best company. I looked up at Tucker. His eyes were closed. I put a hand on his nipple and rubbed it gently.

"Oh fuck!" Tucker liked it.

"Hey, keep your faggot hands off my boy!"

This was dangerous and twisted. I had to stay calm and let their play reach the final act. All three of them were inside me, but somehow it was only me who was the faggot. Men like this were "perverted". They weren't comfortable with what their bodies wanted.

Luckily, Tucker's young cock was a hair trigger. Just touching his chest made the salty-sweet juice drip onto my tongue. He grabbed my head and held himself all the way inside, jerking violently. "Shit! Oh fuck! Oh, Dad!" He didn't finish his thought until after a nonstop flood of cum rushed toward my stomach. "Oh, Dad, you were right."

Curly grunted. "Good. You're gonna have to do that for me now."

Tucker stood up, and I could see the strange union of the two friends in my ass. When I lifted my head to get a better look, Curly shifted forward and covered my eyes, pushing my head down. He kept my eyes covered for the remainder of his performance.

Deprived of sight, I actually began to enjoy the slippery battle between the two giant cocks in my ass. One pushed ahead, then the other, sliding against my insides and each other. I was loosened up enough that the pain had long since subsided, replaced by ecstasy. I looked at Curly, his dad body prickled with sweat. His belly shook with each rough slam. I could only see the outline of Grant; he was the one fucking faster. The two cocks were out of phase; every so often, they joined together and stretched me hard. It was glorious.

Between Curly's fingers, I could see Tucker beside the bed, watching Grant and his dad. His young boner was stiff and stuck straight out. He put his hand around it and stroked.

"No!" Curly barked at his son. "No jacking off."

This was a weird scene. What Dad brings his adult son and best friend to a gay orgy? Why would his rules say it's okay to fuck a man but not to jack off? I was treading on thin ice with this crowd. It felt like any minute, it could go from consensual sex to something much worse. I was still turned on, don't get me wrong, but I was very aware of how fragile the peace was. It could escalate into conflict with one wrong move.

I thought maybe Grant was less repressed than Curly, so I gingerly stretched and rubbed his ass with my toe. I heard him suck air. He sped up a little, so I kept massaging his butt with the soft base of my toe. It worked. He pounded me with increasing strength until I heard his breath change to that familiar final sound.

"Shit, Curly, I'm gonna come!"

Curly said, "Put a finger in my ass, I'm almost there." I thought he was talking to Grant until he grabbed my hand and shoved it in the crack. I put a finger in his hole.

"Ooh yeah. Right there. Just like that."

Grant couldn't hold it any longer. "Ah, shit! Ah fuck! I'm coming!"

He filled me with his hillbilly cum. It made the track a lot more slippery for Curly.

"Oh god. Oh, man." Curly pounded so fast; I could barely hear a gap between the loud smacks of his hips against my ass. He lifted his hand from my eyes, and I saw him kissing Grant. Tucker was looking out the window. He was very hard, rubbing his cock against the windowsill.

I caught his attention and motioned him over. He put his cock back in my mouth. He came immediately.

Curly watched his son blast a hot load in my mouth, and it sent him over the edge. He threw his head back and let out a whoop. "Yeah! That's my boy! Oh man, I'm coming!"

My ass was already stuffed full, and the new blast of cum went beyond capacity. Cum sprayed out of my ass, past Grant's softening cock, and onto the bed. Curly pulled out quickly, bringing the rest of the white river with him. I withdrew my stinky finger from his ass.

I lay on the bed like a leaky pipe, dripping cum from both ends. Grant zipped up, buttoned his shirt, and left without so much as a backward glance.

Curly looked at me sternly. "You should be ashamed

of yourself." I bit my tongue. It was better not to argue. He sauntered out of the room, leaving me with his son.

Tucker looked at me, curled his lip, and said, "Faggot!"

Alone in the room, I thought just how little appreciation a bottom gets. Deckard was an exception. He was eternally grateful for someone with my skills. I thought about Curly leaning back and kissing Grant. Why does he think I'm a 'faggot' and he's not? Asshole.

13
EARL IN ROOM 115

I was too filthy to go to bed, so I returned to the showers. It was pretty late in trucker time. I was alone in there. But when I had my eyes shut to keep out the shampoo, I heard someone walk in and turn on the shower across from me. When I could open my eyes, there was a lone trucker with a grey head of hair and a five o'clock shadow. He soaped up and smiled at me, looking down at my insignificant endowment.

"I like 'em small."

I glanced down and saw a soft, plump, pink penis hanging to the left. It was a bit wrinkled, which, I know, means it's a grower. He studied me while I checked him out.

"Name's Earl."

"Hugh."

The old man grinned. "That was my pa's name. You care to join me for a beer, Hugh?"

I studied his powder blue eyes. There was kindness hiding behind them. "Yeah, that'd be nice."

"I got some bottles of Miller High Life on ice. Room 115."

He soaped up the five o'clock shadow until it was foamy. He took out a safety razor and used his fingers to find his way to a clean shave. Then he soaped up his balls and shaved them, too.

I left him there and put on my pajamas. I nearly fell asleep standing up, but when I heard him turn off the shower, I counted to twenty and headed to his room.

He answered the door naked. He pulled my waist and hauled me into the room, slamming the door. We kissed, and I watched his soft, plump cock grow into a throbbing, veiny monster.

Wordlessly, he reached around and put a hand in my sore asshole. It was soft, like Deckard's. His fingers entered easily, and I heard him grunt with pleasure. He wasted no time, twirling me around and sticking it in. I bent forward onto the bed to give him more traction. He slid in like a foot in a slipper. I hadn't lost count yet, but this was the sixth dick going into one of my holes. There was so much leftover cum up there that I didn't need lubricant.

Earl said, "You're wet up there, son."

"Sorry."

"No, it's nice. Like a woman. But more handsome." He popped the cap on a bottle of "The Champagne of Beers" and handed it to me. I hadn't realized how thirsty I was. I guzzled the beer while we fucked nice and easy. I was so loose now; Earl's fat cock barely touched the sides. He was long enough to hit bottom but didn't pound that wall. My bladder was thankful.

"Kid, you're so loose it's like fucking a sheep."

I laughed. "How would you know?"

Earl guffawed and slapped my ass playfully. I wriggled in response. He slapped it again. It made my insides vibrate. Soon I was churning inside, massaging his cock with my innards. He paddled me over and over, loving how good it felt when I clamped down each time.

I finished my beer and put it down on the bedside table. My head was fuzzy. I didn't often drink, so one beer was enough to make me feel that buzzing in my ears.

"You want another?"

"Yeah, thanks, Earl."

My bottom was chafing under his blows, but it felt too good to stop. He'd had years of experience making men and probably women feel good with that big cock. He knew not to just plow into me and pound. He wasn't gentle, but he wasn't brutal either.

I drank the second beer while we had long, slow sex. Two beers always make me a bit dizzy. I lay my head on the bedspread and moaned quietly. "Earl, you are one talented buttfucker."

Earl laughed. "You make it easy."

I forgot how tired I was when I checked in. Resting my head on the bed, I drifted in and out of a drunken dream. I felt Earl's hands hold my waist as he picked up the pace. He was quiet as a church mouse when he came.

He whispered, "Yeah, boy, sweet. Oh, so sweet."

I held my dick between my thumb and forefinger and stroked a few times, cumming the last drops I could give.

"Earl, you're so hot. Fuck."

14

KENTUCKY TROOPER

The next thing I remember, the dawn light was streaming into the room. I saw the alarm clock read 5:30 am. I was nestled in the crook of Earl's arm. He smiled at me.

"Hey, wanna get breakfast?"

It was nearly four hours to Bowling Green without traffic. I would have to break the speed limit to make it there in time. I leaped up.

"I'm sorry, man. I gotta unstrap at 9:00 am, and it's four hours away."

I hugged him hard and then rushed back to my room. The bed looked like a hundred snails had crawled across it. I wiped it with a washcloth, but it was a disaster. I tore off the bedspread and threw it in the corner. That way, they'd wash it.

I used a washcloth to clean out my bum, threw on a change of clothes, and ran out to my truck. I fired it up and tore out of the motel parking lot. I forgot I had a five-dollar key deposit. Shit. I was going to have to eat that one.

I tore down 71 toward Louisville. I made good time, and by the time I'd gotten through Louisville traffic and took the 65, it was 7:15 am. I'd made back fifteen minutes. I had to keep hightailing it down the interstate to make 9:00 am. In the middle of fucking nowhere, a Kentucky State Policeman siren sounded. FUCK! It was useless. I had screwed up. I pulled over, pounding my fists on the steering wheel.

The young trooper wandered up to the truck. They grow them big in Kentucky. His ass looked like he dined exclusively on Fried Chicken, but his body was a massive, inverted triangle sitting on top of two legs. The seams of his pants were taut, threatening to burst if he flexed a muscle.

"In a hurry?"

I turned red. "Yeah, new job, and I messed up."

"What's your destination, Sir?" He took out a notepad and scribbled something.

"Bowling Green."

"Gotta be there at 8:00, huh?"

I frowned. "No, 9:00."

The trooper laughed. "Bowling Green's Central time, Sir."

I smacked my forehead. "Thank God. Write me the ticket, then. I've got time."

We both laughed. He put the notepad away. "I can let you off on a warning, but, uh, I might need a favor." He adjusted his crotch.

"Anything. What do you need?"

He pointed to the woods off the shoulder. It was just a bunch of trees that didn't belong to anyone. "Come with me."

We walked a few trees deep, and the road disappeared. He pushed me onto my knees and pulled out an average-sized hardon. It was perfectly sculpted, worthy of Michelangelo. I put the tasty treat in my mouth. I swear it tasted like fried chicken.

I put my hands on his bouncy fat butt. It was hairless and soft. I played with it while I engulfed his little dick. He started breathing heavily. I was grateful this little guy had a hair trigger.

"Praise Jesus. Praise Jesus!" He blasted a big load in my mouth. I swished it around and swallowed.

He stared. "You ain't gonna spit?"

I opened my mouth. "Empty. All gone."

That was breakfast.

Back on the road, I was just forty minutes from Bowling Green. My watch said 9:00 am, but in Bowling Green, it was 8:00. I exited the highway and found my way to the drop-off. It was a coal liquefaction plant. It smelled like cancer.

After I unstrapped, I went into the office for coffee and maybe some donuts. The coffee was fresh, and the donuts were deliciously greasy. I ate two.

I found a pay phone and called Mack.

"Hey, Hugh. How was it?"

"Easy." I lied.

"Good. I got a pickup in Virginia tomorrow morning at 9:00 am. Leave the trailer there and head straight to Richmond. It's about 12 hours if you don't stop. You can get a room or whatever and make it by morning."

"Where's it going?"

"Pittsburgh. Lucky, right?"

"I can drop off the trailer if it's better for you."

Mack said, "Leave it there. I'll have our Louisville hub pick it up. Columbus would add three or four hours, and you'd have to cross the mountains. You wouldn't get in until after midnight. I can't have you driving like that. Not on your first run."

"Oh, cool. Deckard kinda explained it to me, but I didn't realize it was that easy."

"Call me when you're in Pittsburgh. I got your check for your training."

"Can I ask how much it is?"

He hung up before I started my sentence.

I got back in my truck, not waiting for the forks to unstrap the load. The further I got from the plant, the healthier I felt. The foul air still left a bitter taste in my mouth.

15

STA-WAKE WITH
PASTOR MIKE

I drove south to Nashville and stopped for gas and breakfast at a huge truck stop on the ring road near the Grand Ole Opry. I avoided eye contact with men. The last thing I needed was sex. Nashville was the coolest city in the South. The people eating in the dining room looked like they could have lived in New York City or Hollywood. The men and the women both wore sunglasses inside, with cowboy shirts, tight jeans, and cowboy boots.

After placing my order (Bacon, eggs, toast, biscuits, gravy, and grits), I went to the travel store. I picked up a city map of Richmond, Nashville, and Knoxville just to be safe. The mileage chart in the back of my Road Atlas said it was 620 miles from Nashville to Richmond. That was a nine-hour drive. I checked my watch. It was 11:00 am. I spent ten minutes plotting my route in my notebook. Nine hours with an hour for pit stops and dinner meant I'd get to Richmond around 9:00 at night. There were no cities between Knoxville and Richmond, so driving all the way through made sense. When I went to pay for my maps, I saw they were selling a box of pills called "Sta-Wake."

I asked the cashier if he'd tried them.

He said, "Last time I took two of those, I woke up

three days later in an alley bleeding out my ass. They're pretty good."

I laughed. "Yeah, but do they work?"

He said, "For the first two days, yeah." They only cost a dollar, so I bought some. I took one. I figured it would wear off when I was ready to sleep. I figured wrong.

The road to Knoxville was hectic. About thirty minutes after taking that pill, I started to feel really good. It got better and better until I felt too good. I had perfect focus. I chewed my tongue. Knoxville was a blur. There were still 450 miles to go. My mind hopped from topic to topic like a frog jumping lily pads. The green forest was especially green. The small towns I passed through looked beautiful. I started making plans to buy a house in Johnson City and move there with Deckard. Deckard! I missed him. The sun set. It was just 100 miles to Richmond. I hadn't stopped. I checked the gas gauge and groaned. I would have to get gas in Charlottesville, VA. When I pulled into the pump, the truck shuddered. I saw the red light indicating the tank was completely empty. I shrugged.

After filling up, I headed towards a sign that read, "Hot Showers."

I paid for my towel and climbed the stairs to the shower room. There was no attendant in sight. The room was small. I found a working showerhead, closed my eyes, and let the water beat on my head.

Someone tapped me on the shoulder. "Hey buddy, you okay?"

"Yeah, why?"

"You're still in your clothes."

I laughed. He didn't join in. He said, "Been hitting the amphetamines?"

I shook my head. "It was called 'Sta-Wake.'"

The guy shook his head. "That's pure Dexedrine.

You're high as a fuckin' kite. They sell that shit in Nashville but not here. You gonna turn off the shower?"

I turned off the shower. I peeled off my soaking wet clothes, wrung them out, and hung them on the towel hook. My hands and legs were shaking. I was fucked up. I screwed up again.

I sat on the floor naked and cried into my hands. The same guy came back. This time, I actually looked at him. He had red curly hair, a mustache, a fat freckled chest, love handles, and a fire crotch. His dick looked pretty plain.

"You want to sleep it off in my truck?"

I looked him up and down. "Yeah, that'd be cool. Thanks."

I put on my soaking-wet jeans and wrapped my upper body in the towel. We walked to his Peterbilt truck.

"Let's get you out of those clothes." He had a whole bedroom in the back of his cab. He took my clothes and hung them above the heater.

I was used to men asking me to take my clothes off. It always meant one thing; they wanted to fuck me. I put my face in the mattress and lifted my ass in the air.

"What the hell you doin'?"

"You don't want to fuck me?"

"No!"

The silence felt like the air was made of split pea soup. I rolled onto my back and covered myself.

"I know you ain't thinkin' straight, so I'm gonna give you a pass. We're gonna sing God's praise together."

"Hymns? That oughta put me to sleep."

He pulled out a colossal hymnal and turned to a random page.

"Sing with me:"

> *I know that my redeemer lives.*
> *Glory Hallelujah!*

> *What comfort this sweet sentence gives!*
> *Glory Hallelujah!*
> *Fight on, pray on; we're gaining ground.*
> *Glory Hallelujah!*
> *The dead's alive, and the lost is found.*
> *Glory Hallelujah!*

He said each line fast, then sang it slow so I could follow along. By the end of the second Glory Hallelujah, I could sing along. It was a miracle. He had hundreds of songs in there.

"Are we singing the whole book?"

"Maybe twenty songs. My name's Pastor Mike, by the way."

"Pastor Mike? I'm Hugh. Hugh Jayness."

"Pleased to make your acquaintance. Now let's sing Idumea."

We went on singing for several hours until I fell asleep.

When I woke up, the sun was cresting the foothills.

Pastor Mike said, "Praise be. The music set you free."

He wasn't lying. I was okay. Was my job OK?

"Where am I?"

"Charlottesville."

"How far to Richmond?"

Pastor Mike scratched his head. "Less than an hour if you're quick."

"What time is it?"

"5:30 am, Hugh. And I'm going to have breakfast. Care to join me? Your clothes are dry." He handed me a neatly folded pile of clothes.

16

MAKING UP FOR LOST TIME

I paid for Mike's breakfast and left at 6:30. I got to the pick-up site at 8:30. They were happy to see me there early. I hitched up and then spent a few minutes studying the Road Atlas. There were thousands of different ways to get from Richmond to Pittsburgh. Most of them passed through the Blue Ridge Mountains on windy roads. With a 40-foot trailer, I couldn't risk it. I had to stay on the main highways. That meant I had to go all the way to Maryland on the 95 and 270, then drive west-northwest to Pittsburgh on three or four more main highways. The best I could estimate it would take six hours, maybe longer if I hit DC traffic. It was going to be tight for a 4:00 pm drop-off. I made notes in my notepad about the drop-off point. I knew Pittsburgh pretty well, but this industrial area was new to me.

The Sta-Wake from last night had depleted some brain chemicals. I was drowsy. The last thing I wanted to do was take another one, so I loaded up on coffee when I stopped for lunch at Grandma's Truck Stop in Hagerstown. The load I was carrying was just under my capacity. I did some calculations, and it looked like I had about ten minutes to eat, drink three cups of coffee, hit the restroom, and get back on the road. I was nervous about the bathroom. I could see the guys going in; they were all good-looking. I walked in, made a bee-line for a stall, and sat down. Just my luck, I went to grab toilet paper and grabbed a huge black dick instead. There was a giant hole cut in the stall wall, and I had somehow failed to notice it on my way in. I tugged twice and said, "Gotta run."

Back in the truck, I navigated the many highways leading to Pittsburgh. I got to the site a few minutes late. The foreman tapped his watch. "You ain't getting paid. You're late."

I knew better than to start a fight. Instead, I took a different approach. I stared at his crotch while I talked to him. "Are you sure there's nothing I can do to make up for it?"

I saw his hand drift to the bulge in his jeans. He adjusted it. "We might be able to work something out."

We went to his office. He closed the blinds, locked the door, and unbuttoned his pants. It was the kind of dick I liked to suck: sort of fat but not too long, maybe six inches. It was throbbing hard; it looked like his wife had neglected it for some time. I got on my knees, but he shook his head. He pulled me up by my armpits and bent me over the desk, roughly sliding my pants down.

He spit in his hand, slicked up his cock, and stuck it in me. Before this week, I probably would have screamed. But after the marathon sessions with Deckard, the double dicking in Cincinnati, and the two times with Mack, I was loose and ready.

He shoved hard, hoping to hear me scream. I didn't want to disappoint him, so I pretended it hurt.

"Ow! Ow! No! Stop!"

"You want me to stop?" It was a rhetorical question. "I ain't stopping, so just forget it. Now take it, little faggot."

Face down on the desk, I rolled my eyes and sighed. "Yes, sir."

I'd forgotten what it felt like to have such a normal-sized dick inside me. It wasn't enough. I'd been ruined. I did my best to enjoy it but didn't even get hard.

"You want me to shoot my load in you?"

"Yes. Yes."

"What's the magic words?"

"Please, sir. Please shoot your load in me."

He was one of those assholes who got off on feeling powerful by yanking everyone's leash.

"Here it comes." His announcement was a bit early. He kept fucking for another ten minutes and finally left a lackluster load in me.

When I returned to the truck, the load was un-strapped, and I headed to Avalon Trucking. Mack was just about to lock up.

"There you are. Come on in."

I folded my arms. "Okay if I just wait here?"

He eyed me. "Don't worry, I won't fuck you now. It's closing time."

I didn't know if I believed him but I went in anyway.

He unlocked his top desk drawer and pushed an en-velope over to me.

It was a bank check. I was going to have to get an account. It was time I grew up a little. The check was for $285.00. It was more money than I'd made all year. I felt a surge of that giddy payday energy.

"Good feeling, right?" He winked at me.

I saw that he was rubbing his crotch. The money was so good, I didn't care.

"Let's fuck, Mack. Let's celebrate."

He said, "I suppose the Missus can wait a little longer."

He wanted me to blow him first. He leaned back against the desk, opened his fly, and let the massive meat rise towards the ceiling.

It was too tight. I felt the corners of my mouth

stretch until they cracked. I wouldn't be able to smile for a week. But I blew him. He wanted in all the way, so he pushed my head down onto him until he passed my tonsils. I couldn't breathe. I had to pound his leg to get him to release me.

"Let's fuck."

He stayed leaning on the desk, his massive butt covering the blotter paper. I dropped my pants. He picked me up high until I was centered over his pole. Then I slid down the pole like a fireman in slow motion. I leaned left and let him into my colon.

"Oh, fuck that feels good, Hugh. You know, you're the only one who–"

I clamped a hand over his mouth. "Don't speak. Fuck."

He stood up, holding me by the armpits, and began to fuck hard. It felt good to have a real cock inside me. Deckard was the best, of course, but Mack was way better than that asshole foreman.

"You like that, boy?"

I nodded. "Mm-hmm."

"You like it when Daddy fucks you?"

"Yes, Daddy, fuck me, Daddy."

He threw me down on the desk, rotating me so I landed on my back. He was powerful, a master of ass fucking. I put my hands on his huge muscular butt cheeks. I could feel the glutes tighten as he thrust. Despite being hairy all over his chest, arms, and legs, his butt cheeks were smooth. I rubbed like I was trying to get a genie to come out of them. I reached up and pinched a furry nipple.

"Oh, man! Keep doing that, and I'll be home in time for supper."

I played with both tits at the same time. Big droplets of sweat cascaded off his forehead, hitting me in the face and neck. The musky scent was intoxicating.

I licked his sweaty arm. My mouth filled with the taste of a pretzel on a locker room floor.

Mack got so excited that he kept missing the second hole and pounding my bladder instead. A little pee escaped. I leaned and shifted so he was back in all the way. The fat head stretched my inner hole, which brought Mack to orgasm.

"Oh god. Oh, Hugh. Oh shit." He jerked and held me against his chest. I licked a nipple, and he unleashed a torrent inside me. We stayed like that. No kissing, no affection, just me licking his nipple as he held my head to his chest. He let me go. He dropped a large manila envelope on the floor and centered it under my plugged hole. When he withdrew, his semen spilled out of me in rivulets, tickling my balls before dripping onto the envelope. When the trickle stopped, he folded the envelope in four and tossed it in the wastebasket.

"I hope it's not fish. We're not even Catholic." Mack buttoned and buckled. We walked out together.

"It's a slow day tomorrow. I'll let you catch up on some sleep. If Deckard lets you, that is."

I smiled. "Where is he?"

"He went to Harrisburg. Should be home soon."

17

HOME COMING

Deckard was standing on the front porch smoking a cigarette when I pulled up. He saw me limping and laughed.

"Did you just come from the office?"

I held up the envelope, "Almost 300 smackeroos."

"Judging by the way you're walking, he broke his Friday rule."

I smiled. "Yeah, he said there wouldn't be any sex. But he lied."

Deckard drew in a long puff. "Should I be jealous?"

I shook my head. "He's going home to his wife. You got me anytime you want now."

Deckard raised an eyebrow. "Really?" He massaged his jeans. I hoped the neighbors weren't watching. "Why don't you come inside and wash up? I'll make some spaghetti."

After supper, we sat on the couch watching reruns of Ben Casey, MD.

Deckard wrapped a muscular, protective arm around my shoulders. I leaned my head on his bicep. He flexed, making my head bob up and down. We laughed. I looked into his eyes, and we kissed.

Clothing came off quickly. We were naked in the living room. I lay on the gray sofa, lifting my legs and holding them up with my arms. I used my hands to spread my butt cheeks and showed off my hole, which opened and closed like a goldfish's mouth. Deckard greased up his long fat pole and wiped the excess inside my ass. I'd never dated a guy before, so I didn't know about the bicycle effect. My ass had learned to take Deckard, and it didn't forget. He entered me as smoothly as if he were just regular size. I think it's partly your body's muscle memory but also the relaxing feeling of being with someone you trust. I think maybe it's love, too. The pain was nowhere to be found. He pushed up inside me until I had that sensation of being as full as possible. Even when his heavy balls smacked my butt, it felt familiar and safe. I held his bottom with both hands and pushed him into me hard.

The kissing had a nice effect. Even though Deckard was rock hard, he swelled up another inch around when we kissed. That pressure sent me into spasms that massaged Deckard's cock. I bucked like a rodeo bull. The bucking was all involuntary, fueled by passion, and forged in the fire of lust.

Deckard was past words. His eyes were half shut. We kissed for ten-minute stretches, then took breaks to get our breath. Deckard was nowhere near climax, and that was how I wanted it. I could fuck until December.

Silently, he wrapped his arms around my lower back and lifted me into the air. He fucked me from below as he carried me into the bedroom. There, he lay me on my side and lifted one leg. It was a new position for us. It gave him at least two more inches of easy access. That meant his cock head suddenly smacked into the wall of my descending colon. I nearly fainted from the intense pleasure. Shockwaves came out, intensifying the spasms and increasing their frequency. If pleasure were poison, I'd have died.

The sensation of hitting another wall was the tipping point for Deckard. He pounded there over and over, grunting, leaving me soaked in beads of sweat from his brow. I twisted my torso and clamped my mouth on his nipple, swirling my tongue over it.

"Oh fuck, Hugh, I'm gonna come."

Just hearing those words, my own little dick decided to pop off. In a spectacular arc, my cum shot across the king-sized bed and landed on the opposite wall. Then I felt it. His balls were touching my ass. I couldn't see, but I could feel them clenching and unclenching, so even before I felt the milky warm mess inside, I knew it was churning its way towards me. Like a bee stinger, his balls throbbed a dozen times before they descended. Without withdrawing, Deckard got into a spoon with me. We stayed like that, his massive cock inside me, until we both fell asleep.

18

MISSIONARY

The next day, Deckard had morning wood. He was still inside me. It was such a surprising turn-on; it only took twenty strokes before he shot his load. It's a good thing, too, because he had to be in Erie at 9:00 am. He was going to drop off in Buffalo, meaning I would have the house to myself for a day. I wanted to see Niagara Falls, but I had to stay by the phone in case a last-minute job came in.

Deckard whistled "Fifteen Miles on the Erie Canal" while he showered. He kissed me on the way out the door. It was 6:30 am. It was a two-hour drive up the 79. Buffalo was only one-and-a-half hours from Erie. He had an easy day.

"I have to sit on the load until 2:30 pm. Means I'll be home by 7:00."

"I'll be here unless Mack calls. What do you want for dinner? Lasagna?"

Deckard rubbed his belly. "Sounds good."

I heard his truck start, and he pulled away. I took off all my clothes and walked around the house naked. That's just the normal thing to do in this situation. I watched the news naked, too. The doorbell rang.

"Shit." I put on my jeans and undershirt as fast as I

could. The doorbell rang again. I opened it to see two pink-faced young men in suits. Mormons.

"Hello, sir. I'm Elder Pruitt, and this is Elder Granger. We'd like to talk to you about a Gospel-centered lifestyle."

I never slam doors in people's faces. I know they think they're saving souls, and I don't want to make their life any more pointless than it already is. I felt mischievous, though.

"Sure. Do you drink lemonade?" Mormons can't have caffeine.

Elder Granger spoke. "Yes, sir, we do. Appreciate it."

"Well, come in."

They left their bicycles on the porch. I led them to the kitchen table. We chattered away while I made pink lemonade from the freezer.

"You boys from around here?"

"No, sir. We're from Idaho. Coeur d'Alene."

"You're a long way from home. Do you miss your families?"

Pruitt said, "Not yet. We just started our mission."

I looked at Granger. "Do you like Pittsburgh?"

Neither of them said a word. I laughed. "It probably feels like Sodom and Gomorrah coming from Idaho."

They laughed in that way that says they're not supposed to laugh at scripture. Granger shifted in his seat, suddenly revealing an impressive bulge in his slacks. I poured them lemonade. I couldn't see Pruitt's bulge at all. I think he might have gotten the Jayness genes. I wondered if they had met in camp, chosen each other for the mission, and were secretly getting it on. I doubted I'd ever know.

When they finished the lemonade, they turned the talk back towards the strange scripture of the Book of Mormon.

"Do you believe God has a plan for you?" Granger

looked at me with doe eyes, hoping he'd found a new investigator.

"He does, and it's not at all what you'd expect."

Pruitt wrinkled his nose. "I don't follow."

"God made me homosexual."

Their eyes darted nervously around the room. Granger said, "That's okay. As long as you don't act on those impulses and follow his word."

"I act on them every day. Sometimes two or three times a day."

They both stood up abruptly. Granger's bulge was pulsing through the fabric.

"What did you put in the lemonade?" Pruitt pointed a finger at me.

"Frozen lemonade and water."

Granger adjusted his hard-on and limped towards the door. "Thank you for the hospitality. I pray you find God's real plan."

I said, "Be sure to talk to your pastor about this. I doubt I'm your first and certainly won't be your last."

Pruitt marched out onto the porch, but Granger stayed on the threshold. "I'm sorry to trouble you, sir, but could I use the bathroom?"

"Last door on the left."

Pruitt shouted, "Come on, man. It's the house of the devil."

Granger said, "Wait on the sidewalk."

I closed the front door. Granger pushed me into the kitchen and forced me onto the floor. He whipped out his fat pink cock. It was throbbing and veiny. There were tears in his eyes.

"God, please forgive me. And forgive Hugh, too." Granger pressed his cock to my lips. I looked up at his apple cheeks and pasty face. I opened my mouth. He held my hair to steady my head and humped in and out. He was a natural, but I don't think he knew he could go deeper. I held his waist in case touching his butt would freak him out, and I pushed him all the way in until his balls brushed my chin.

I must have blown his young mind. His eyes were salad plates. He immediately shot a month's worth of cum. It overflowed onto my chin, my undershirt, and my jeans. Then, more came out. And more. Puddles formed on the kitchen floor. Shadows haunted Granger's expression. Hell was very real for him.

I wiped my mouth, swallowing what I could. Granger stepped away, zipping up.

He ran out the door and down the steps. I heard Pruitt say, "What took you so long?"

"Shut up. I was making a BM."

I watched them as they made their way down the street. I wondered if Granger wanted Pruitt to perform a similar service for him. It would make life on the road a lot easier.

19

BETTER

I drove to the A&P and picked up crushed tomatoes, Italian herbs, lasagna noodles, hot sausage, hamburger, mozzarella cheese, and a few secret ingredients. I got it assembled and put it in the oven at 6pm.

I stepped out on the porch for a smoke. The neighborhood was nicer than anywhere I'd ever lived. The lawns were kept neatly trimmed. The flower beds were full of seasonal annuals. The cars were recent models; they had all their wheels. Just then I saw Deckard's truck round the corner. He flashed his lights and waved.

I had a moment of clarity. I was on the threshold of a new, better life. Instead of lonely rooming houses and odd jobs, I had a home, a man, and a good job. Seeing that man approach the house, I was overcome with a warm, safe feeling. He got out of the truck.

"Hey Hugh!"

I waved and quickly covered my eyes. I had no reason to cry. They must have been tears of joy.

He ran to my side, putting an arm around my shoulder. "You okay, buddy?"

I nodded, sniffed. "I don't know what this feeling is."

"Describe it."

"Well, I felt safe when I saw you. And when you got out of the truck, I don't know, I felt warm. I'm not sad, I'm just crying for no reason."

Deckard grinned. "That sounds like love."

EPILOGUE

I don't know what I did to deserve him, but I thank my lucky stars we met. It's been six years since we got together. One thing that's really helped our relationship last so long is that we don't follow the rules of monogamy.

It's pretty easy to make it work. Two men, two male libidos, we need a little variety. Don't misunderstand: Deckard is my main man, and I'm his. But when we drive separately, we play separately. And when we drive together, we play together. Think about it, and it makes sense. I'm too small to give Deckard the fucking he deserves. He's too big for me to blow. We have to fill in the gaps somehow.

We mostly drive together now. We earned so much money between us, with no kids or wives to spend it all. We started a savings account, bought some T-bills, and watched it grow.

We got a stockbroker who helped us grow our savings into a vast fortune. He put half of it in gold and the rest in the 'ampersand' stocks: Procter & Gamble, Johnson & Johnson, AT&T. Now our money pays us money every month.

We still do plenty of driving, but we usually drive together like that first time when we fell in love. We stop at truck stops and play with other men. There are some guys we see so regularly, they're practically part of our family. In the showers, I look for the guys who are somewhat above average. Perfect for sucking dick. Deckard looks for the even bigger guys. I love watching him smile when he takes one of the giants. I'll admit, when the playing together started, my self-esteem took a hit. I wanted to fuck him and make him happy like that. But I saw the way he looked when I was giving head. I'm sure he wanted to be smaller, so I could do that with him. But whether I'm too small for some things and he's too big for others, we still satisfy each other in so many ways. Truck stop showers are where we fill in the gaps.

Our wealth has given us freedom. Each time we strap on a new load, it's a new adventure. We don't drive for a living. We live to drive.

IV

FIREHOUSE LOVERS

THE NEW RECRUIT

Travis Baumholt tried twice before he passed the written firefighter exam. He had to live at home with his parents while he waited between tests and for the six-month waiting period before he finally would be assigned to a station.

Living at home was becoming a nightmare. Travis had to listen to his father complain about the "freaks and queers" moving into the Castro District in San Francisco. His parents moved to the Castro when it was a mostly Italian borough. Travis's mother was of Italian descent, and since she did all the cooking, it was wise to live closer to the markets where she could get fresh pasta, San Marzano tomatoes, and Arborio rice for risotto. His conservative parents watched their neighborhood change into a paradise for homosexuals. They didn't know that Travis had developed a longing to be with other men. Every time his father said, "faggot," or "queer," Travis died inside a little.

Despite being of Italian and German heritage, Travis had pulled the short straw in the genetic lottery. God gifted him a handsome face, a trim waist, and heart-shaped buttocks, but he was ruthless when he gave him a tiny penis. It was a source of deep shame. He didn't know how two men were "queer" together, but he was sure his little dick would be a problem. He had only seen one homoerotic drawing in his life, an image by the artist Tom of Finland: two men with huge cocks. One man penetrated the anus of the other, who held his colossal shaft with a look of joy. Travis felt woefully inadequate ever since seeing that lone image of homosexual coupling.

Day after day, Travis waited for his assignment. He was too frightened to walk inside the taverns along Castro where the fairies met. If he had, he might have learned that size wasn't the only currency in the gay world. But his fear kept him from that knowledge. One day in June, one of the few warm days in the otherwise foggy, cold city, a letter arrived. To his astonishment, his assignment was only a few blocks from his parent's house at Fire Station 24 on Hoffman Street. It was a tiny station, just a few men and one engine. The firehouse was perched at the lower end of Diamond Heights, with an incredible panoramic view of the city and the bay. It was so close that he could quickly get there from his parent's house. His shift was 24 hours, which meant he got to sleep at the station overnight before returning home. It was his first time living apart from his parents for any length of time, and he couldn't wait to pack a bag and stay there.

So the next day, he did just that. His mother offered to pay for a taxicab, but he preferred the gentle, sometimes steep walk uphill to the firehouse. He found a locked door when he arrived at the station at noon. He knocked.

A seasoned older man opened the door. His hair was salt and pepper to match his close-cropped beard. His blue eyes twinkled when he saw Travis.

"You must be the new guy. I'm Petey McBride." The older man extended a large, veiny hand.

"Travis. Travis Baumholt, sir."

Petey smiled. "Let me show you your bunk. You got

big shoes to fill. Shep moved up the hill last week. He was a youngster like you. You're rooming with his buddy Mike."

They walked through the empty garage. Where was the fire truck?

Petey read Travis's mind. "They're out on a call. Not a fire, from what I heard. Just a cat in a tree or whatever."

Up the stairs, they arrived at a small room at the front of the station with a great view. The room was small, dominated by a bunk bed.

"Mike prefers the top bunk, even though he's a big guy. I don't know why. So you lucked out. You get the bottom bunk. Much easier when you gotta take a piss in the middle of the night."

Travis surveyed the small room. He was going to be in close quarters with this Mike fellow. He worried his little secret would come out at some point. It would be hard to hide, even though it was so tiny. He'd kept it a secret until senior year when the whole class went on a trip to Clear Lake. There, the boys and girls slept in separate cabins on opposite sides of the lake. So late at night, the boys decided to go skinny dipping. Travis tried to stay behind, but they dragged him to the shore and stripped him. The other boys pointed and laughed.

"It's a fuckin' button!"

"I pity the girl that marries you!"

He could still hear the jeers in his head. It left him feeling hopeless. What guy would ever want to be with him?

"Hey, you still with us?" Petey clapped Travis on the back. "You look like you went to Jupiter for a minute there."

Travis laughed. "Yeah, there's a lot of change all at once. Sorry about that."

Petey got serious. "Don't ever do that in a fire. You'll end up a pile of ashes for us to clean up."

Travis swallowed hard. "Right, sir. Sorry."

Petey smiled. "Enough with the sir. We're all firemen here. I ain't your boss, and you ain't mine. How about we call each other 'brother' from now on? Sound good, brother?"

Travis nodded. "Yes, brother."

Petey said, "The fire chief has us on a synchronous schedule. That means that each 24-hour shift is the same five guys. So you might see some other guys at the change of shift, but this shift, we're a team. If you don't get along and fit in with us, you might get moved to another shift. But you seem like a sweet kid. If you can win over your roommate, you'll be with us for sure."

"I'll do my best."

"Good! I'll leave you to unpack."

Travis found an empty cubby and filled it with his change of clothes. He put his toiletries on the window ledge, hung up his towel on a hook, and he was unpacked. He studied the top of his roommate's cubby. There was a motorcycle helmet, Aqua Velva, shaving cream, a razor (Travis didn't need those yet), and a tub of Vaseline. Travis had no idea what that was for. Maybe Mike had eczema.

Travis wandered through the station, looking at the pictures on the walls. There was a photo of the Hoffman Street station crew at a Fireman's Muster in Golden Gate Park. They were all handsome men. Most sported a thick mustache, making them indistinguishable from the clone-like gays on Castro Street. They huddled together for the camera, arms around each other's necks. It looked like a brotherhood. Travis was an only child and could only imagine what it would be like to have a brother.

The garage door rolled up loudly, and an engine backed in. Three sturdy men clambered down off the truck. Petey made introductions.

"Fellows, this here's Travis. He's brand new, so go easy on him."

A redhead with intense freckles offered his hand. "Keith. Nice to meet you, Travis." Keith didn't smile, but he didn't scowl, either. He was friendly but guarded.

A tall, skinny man with a blond buzz cut gave a big grin. "Travis! Name's Frank, but they call me French Fry. Welcome, brother!" There was that word again. It made Travis feel warm inside.

Travis had to tilt his head back to look French Fry in the eyes. "Damn, you're tall."

French Fry laughed. "Yeah, I know. Skinny, too." He wrapped his giant hand around Travis's as they shook. "I'm long and skinny everywhere."

The last guy to approach had to be Mike. He was not too tall, with brown hair, green eyes, and noticeably bulging biceps.

Travis said, "You must be Mike. We're roommates."

Mike eyed the kid warily. "Good guess, Sherlock." He shook Travis's hand and turned away.

"Nice to meet you, brother!"

Mike shrugged. "Yeah, whatever."

Travis studied his coworkers. Not one of them wore a wedding band. He thought about how hard living away from a family would be. Other than Petey, all these guys were young. Travis found it odd that they had chosen this life over a wife and kids.

"None of you are married?"

The station went silent. Petey spoke up. "This shift is all bachelors. The married firemen have too many distractions, so count your blessings. We all pay close attention and watch out for our brothers. You don't want a married man watching your back. He'll leave you to roast if it means getting back to his wifey and kids."

The others nodded. Mike didn't participate.

French Fry leaned in and whispered in Travis's ear.

"Mike was real close with Shep. He's just taking it hard. Shep was like a father to him."

Travis nodded. "Thanks for filling me in. I thought it was me."

Keith shook his head, joining the conversation. "Nah, he's a stand-up guy. Swell. He'll be cool in a week or two. Just give him room."

As the new guy, Travis had the worst of the dinner chores. He had to peel potatoes and chop onions and was stuck washing the dishes when the lackluster dinner was over. Petey offered to help with the pots and pans, which had become crusted with dry mashed potatoes, caramelized chuck steak, and burnt broccoli.

It was an easy day, but all the new sights and sounds had exhausted Travis. He fell into bed. Mike was reading a book up top.

He leaned his head down. "You don't mind if I keep the light on to read, do you?"

Travis smiled, grateful for his first real interaction with his handsome roommate. "Not at all, Mike."

"Thanks, brother."

Travis fell asleep moments later.

In the middle of the night, the fire bell rang. Travis wasn't ready to fight a fire yet, but he had to join the men in the truck all the same. He didn't even have his uniform, so he wore a dark t-shirt and brown Ben Davis work pants. Just like in the old movies, the men slid down a pole. No time for stairs. They all climbed aboard the truck, and moments later, they were zooming down 20th Street toward a fire near Dolores Park. Travis could see the smoke rising above a burning building.

When they arrived, Keith told Travis to hook up the hose to the hydrant. Travis had practiced it a hundred times, but he nearly froze. Mike came over, cursing him out. "Let me fucking do it! Jesus Christ!"

Travis stepped back and let the hulking man connect the hose. He felt his eyes sting and wiped them to keep tears from falling.

Keith nudged him. "Don't let him get to you. He thinks he's God's gift to the profession."

Travis nodded, afraid his voice would crack if he said anything. French Fry aimed water at the flames. Mike and Keith broke down the front door and ran in to rescue any stragglers. It turned out to be an abandoned apartment building, so there were no heroic rescues that night. After several hours, the last of the embers died. The building was in ruins, but none of the neighboring residences had burned. It was a success.

Back at the station, the men were too amped up to sleep, so they started a poker game. Petey gave his chair to Travis, who didn't know much about the game. They bet nickels, dimes, and quarters. Petey coached Travis, who had beginner's luck and walked away with six dollars after the last round. Mike was pissed, but the other guys clapped Travis on the back and congratulated him.

As the sun rose over Oakland, the men fell into their beds and slept soundly. When he woke up, Travis discovered what Mike used the Vaseline for. He thought maybe there was an earthquake. The bunk was shaking.

The mirror above Mike's dresser gave Travis a view that left him speechless. Mike stroked a dick so big it made Tom of Finland seem realistic. Mike turned his head towards the mirror, checking to be sure Travis was asleep. Travis closed his eyes and pretended to be asleep, but he opened them a crack and kept watching. His hand made its way to his tiny penis, and he rubbed it, excited beyond belief. He came in his underwear in less than a minute and was ready for another round.

Mike was near the end, and his eyes were closed. His tongue licked his mustache as he polished the knob with one hand and stroked up and down the enormous shaft with the other. Travis didn't know why it turned him on so much, but it did. The size just somehow multiplied the sexual energy in the room.

Mike whispered under his breath, "Oh fuck. Oh fuck."

Travis watched as a fountain of cum burst from the top of the enormous fuck stick. It made him come again. His underwear was soaked. Mike grabbed a white washcloth from the bed knob and wiped himself down. He jumped down out of bed, his massive dong swinging like a pendulum.

"Enjoy the show?"

Travis pretended to be sound asleep.

"I saw you watching me, little pervert." Mike threw a towel over his shoulder and walked to the hall shower.

Travis smacked his forehead. "Stupid! Stupid idiot!"

Mike stuck his head back in the room. "I put on a good show, don't I?" He winked. Travis blushed. He waited until Mike was definitely in the shower, then threw his soaked underwear in his bag and put on a clean pair. He wrapped his towel around his waist, making sure to put a lump in the front that kept any prying eyes from figuring out he had nothing much down there.

Mike came out of the shower, steam radiating off his body. "All yours."

Travis locked the bathroom door before hopping into the shower to wash the sperm off. He lathered up his hair, and then someone tried the door handle, then pounded on the door. "Hey, some of us gotta take a dump!"

Travis was mortified. He washed the shampoo out as best he could in three seconds, wrapped the towel around his waist, then opened the door.

"Sorry."

Keith laughed. "You got suds in your hair. Get back in the shower, dude. I'm just gonna take a crap."

Keith put his hand on his hip and waited for Travis to remove the towel. "Don't be shy. You're amongst brothers."

With a groan, Travis removed the towel, exposing his minuscule penis to the redhead. He turned crimson.

Keith smiled. "Sorry, brother. I didn't know."

In solidarity, Keith took off his pants and lowered his underwear. "See, I ain't much to brag about." Keith had red pubic hair and a small, soft dick. It dwarfed Travis's tiny nub, but it wasn't big. "So don't sweat it. I get a lot of compliments 'cause it don't hurt when I put it in 'em. Now, Mike, I pity that guy."

Travis was bewildered by all this sex talk. Even in high school, he'd avoided the topic for fear of being exposed as a homo or, worse, his little secret getting out. Suddenly, he was surrounded by guys who wanted to talk about dicks.

Keith pulled up his pants. "Besides, what you don't have up front, you more than make up for in back. I'd love to fuck that ass."

Travis got hard hearing those words. Not that anyone could tell, really. Keith put a freckled finger between Travis's butt cheeks and swiped it up, holding it to his nose. "Oh, fuck, dude. Sweet."

Travis felt faint and had to sit down. Keith leaned over and whispered in his ear. "Next shift, if nothing is happening, come to my room. I'll show you what that ass is for."

2

THEY DON'T JUST SELL
BOOKS

Travis walked downhill toward his awful parents' house, his head swimming with a maelstrom of sexual fantasy and desire. He couldn't believe he'd have to wait 48 hours to be back with his brothers. The anticipation was killing him.

He passed a bookstore on 19th Street and was surprised by the titles in the window. "Bunkhouse Hunks" and "Lusty Seamen" were just a few of the titles. The drawings on the front were incredibly sexy. The door of the stoor opened, and a lunchtime patron slipped out, giving Travis a quick nod before hurrying down the street. His curiosity was intense. The store's sign said, "Minors Prohibited. 18 Years or Older Only."

California had a strange concept of minors. Travis was old enough to die in a fire or fight a war, but he wasn't old enough to drink or even walk into a gay bar. But he was old enough for this bookstore. His hormones were on fire. He reached a tipping point. "Fuck it," he thought and walked into the store.

A handsome man with a handlebar mustache greeted Travis as he walked in. Travis nodded and turned to the news rack, which held all familiar magazines like Architectural Digest and Gentleman's Quarterly. He'd expected to see dirty magazines, but there were none.

A man emerged from a beaded curtain in the back of the store. He placed a book and a magazine on the counter for purchase. The clerk held up the book. "Peter Schutes, excellent choice!" The man grunted and paid, hurrying out of the shop.

Travis saw the sign above the doorway. It said, "Paradise Books" with a down arrow. He realized there were two bookstores in one storefront. It had taken a great deal of courage to walk into the store. Now he needed even more courage to walk past that beaded doorway. He was a fireman. Could he lose his job? Maybe. Did he care? Not right now. His tiny little dick did all the thinking for him.

He smiled at the shopkeeper and pushed past the curtains. He was glad nobody asked to see his ID. He wanted to remain anonymous. There was a long stairway to a dimly lit basement where the racks of pornography and erotic books were on full display. He'd never seen so many homoerotic images in one place before. His head was swimming. He picked up a magazine called "Inches" and felt dismayed that all the models were huge, giving their precise measurements in their biographies. He looked around in all the magazines but didn't see anyone with his little problem. Maybe he wasn't meant to be a gay man because he was too small down there.

A hand landed on his shoulder. He whirled around to see a moderately handsome middle-aged man with his other hand holding a nice, average cock.

"You like to suck dick, boy?"

Travis looked around nervously. They were the only two men in sight. "I— I never did it before."

The man's eyes narrowed. "You a virgin?"

Travis nodded.

"You lucked out. I'm an expert teacher in the art of cocksucking. Come on."

Travis followed the man past a curtain into a semi-private "reading room" with a bench and table. The man sat on the table, displaying his erect penis. Travis felt horror and fear as he realized he'd taken a one-way trip and could never return. But his loins overpowered his brain. The man held Travis's head and gently lowered it onto his cock. Travis opened his mouth wide and felt the fleshy knob against his tongue and palate.

"Watch the teeth." The man held Travis by the ears and tugged until he was all the way in. Travis gagged. In response, the man lifted Travis partway so that he could recover. He whispered in Travis's ear. "You gotta fight that. Your body thinks it's in control, but you are. You can make it stop if we practice a little first."

True to his word, the man was an excellent teacher. Travis concentrated each time the cock touched his tonsils until, finally, he mastered the gag reflex. It still snuck up on him, but he could control it.

"Now, I'm not that big, but I'm big enough to go deep. You ready?"

Travis nodded. The man held Travis down as he pushed upwards until the head of his cock pushed past the tonsils into his throat. Travis shivered with a rush of pride.

The man said, "You're already a better cocksucker than most guys out there. You got a tight throat."

Travis couldn't say anything. He realized he couldn't breathe. He started to panic and flailed his arms.

The man released him. He came up, coughing and gasping for air. Despite the discomfort, there was powerful electricity coursing through him. It came from his connection with the other man. There was an almost magic quality to the intimacy of oral sex.

"This will be more comfortable. Here, lie on your back." Travis obeyed, lying on the table with his head dangling off the edge. The man held his head gently, like a chiropractor about to make a neck adjustment. But he didn't twist. He put his cock into Travis's mouth and went straight down his throat. He began fucking the boy's face. His hips swiveled, and his breath grew shaky.

"Oh, shit, boy, you're so fucking sexy!" The man's cock gave off a slippery droplet of precum that lubricated Travis's throat. It tasted like clam juice and maple syrup. The man picked up speed, ignoring Travis's retching and gagging. "I'm almost there, boy, don't quit."

Travis wanted to serve the man like a good little boy. He was embarrassed when some of his dinner from the night before came up and filled his mouth with bile. He coughed, and it came out of his nose. It burned. His eyes watered.

"Oh shit, I'm there. I'm coming. I'm coming." The stranger threw his head back and gave a loud grunt. He shoved his cock as deep as he could, forcing his cum down Travis's throat like a feeding tube at the hospital. He pulled out, still shooting, coating Travis's face with thick, ropy cum.

"Thanks, man." The older gentleman zipped up his pants and rushed out of the room. Travis wiped his face with his shirt sleeve. His first time was hot but not very romantic. He needed to get home in time for lunch.

As he rushed down Castro towards his house, he reflected on his first experience. He thought having sex would remove the hollow, empty feeling in his chest, but it didn't. If anything, it made it a little worse. He'd seen enough Hollywood movies to know what it meant to be loved. It wasn't the same as giving a stranger a blow job. It was something more. He knew his parents probably had it once. The way they finished each others' sentences and cracked inside jokes that only they got was the remnants of love. The bitter arguments and long silences were probably some kind of love, too, but it wasn't what he was looking for.

He burst through the door and smelled his mother's bolognese cooking on the stove.

"Travis, that you?"

"Yeah, ma!" He rushed to the bathroom to check his face. He saw dried cum on his sideburns. He wiped them clean with a wash rag.

His mother shouted, "Come eat! It's a getting cold!"

He sat at the table across from his father. His mother laid down steaming plates of spaghetti. His father read the afternoon Examiner and ignored his child.

His mother said, "How was your first shift at work? I heard the sirens last night and thought maybe it was you."

"Yeah, I went to a fire near Dolores Park in the middle of the night."

"I'm so proud of you!" She passed him a cheese grater with a hard block of dry Parmesan. He shaved it while he waited for his father to chime in. The old man shuffled his newspaper and said nothing.

"Dad, did you hear the sirens?"

"Nope." He went back to his paper, utterly disinterested in being a father. Travis fumed inside but kept his anger to himself. It was his first day on the job, and his papa didn't give a shit. He could hardly wait for two days to pass to return to the firehouse and be with his new family of brothers. He counted the seconds.

3

KEITH BREAKS HIM IN

T ravis climbed Alvarado Street, his small knapsack on his shoulder. This time the door to the garage was open, and the men were polishing the engine. He was right on time. Petey handed him a bucket of soapy water and a big sponge.

"Take off your shirt; enjoy the sunshine." It was a nice warm day in Diamond Heights. Usually, June was as cold as January because of the persistent fog, but today was nearly 80 degrees. The other men had their shirts off, too, their muscles flexing as they scrubbed and polished the engine.

By far the most muscular of the five men, Mike looked like a Mr. Universe contestant. His lateral muscles formed wings. His pectoral muscles bounced with each firm stroke of his sponge. He wore cop sunglasses, which made him look even more aloof than he already acted. He caught a glimpse of Travis and tilted his head, cracking a small smile. "Hey, Kid."

Travis felt butterflies in his stomach. He swallowed hard. "Hey, Mike."

The hunky roommate went back to polishing the chrome. He turned, revealing the long log of flesh that crept down his thigh, barely hidden in his baggy Ben Davis trousers. Travis gave an involuntary gasp. He imagined what it would be like trying to choke down that summer sausage. His mouth would barely fit the thing soft. If it got hard, it would break his jaw!

"Hey, wake up, space cadet!" Keith patted Travis on the rear. "When this is over, let's have lunch up in my room. I got dessert waiting for you."

Travis remembered Keith's promise to fuck his ass. He felt his anus pucker with fear and excitement. He headed inside.

When the truck was shiny enough to send a message to Mars, the men went inside and grabbed sandwiches. Keith nodded his head in the direction of the stairs. Travis followed him to the room he shared with French Fry.

"We got this place to ourselves." Keith hung a sock over the doorknob and closed it. "You ever get fucked before?"

Travis shook his head.

Keith grinned. "It hurts, at least at first, but you're gonna like it once I get you warmed up."

Travis worried. His ass hurt just thinking about a dick going in there. He'd tried putting a carrot up there once after seeing that Tom of Finland drawing. It was a small carrot, and it hurt like a motherfucker. He threw it away, and his mother found it in the trash. She scolded him for wasting food and washed it to add to her wedding soup.

"Hey, Kid, are you still there?" Travis had spaced out again. Keith had his pants off, and his modest cock made a tent in his boxer shorts.

"Sorry, I'm here. Wh-what happens next?"

Keith didn't use words to answer. He lifted Travis onto his bunk and put the younger man's legs on his shoulders. He leaned forward and licked Travis's butthole.

"You like that?"

Travis nodded. "It's good."

"It's gonna get a lot better." Keith used his tongue like a conductor might use a baton. He licked, spit, stretched, sucked, and slurped. Travis couldn't believe how good it felt.

"Oh shit, Keith. Oh god."

Keith pulled back with a big wet grin. "I know, right?" He returned to his task, leaving Travis in a whirlwind of pleasant sensations. His tiny dick was stiff and wet. He didn't dare touch it for fear it would explode.

Keith stopped and stood, rubbing some baby oil on his cock. He poured a little into his hand and wiped it on Travis's backside. He stuck an oily finger in the wet butthole and twirled it around.

Travis squeaked. It hurt a little.

"You okay?"

By the time Keith asked, it had stopped hurting and started to feel good. Keith was tapping on a spot in there that felt like a joy buzzer. "It's good, Keith. Keep going."

The redhead pulled out his finger, then went in with two, using them like chopsticks to stretch the boy's hole wider.

Travis pounded the mattress. He knew the pain was going to subside, but it didn't make it hurt any less.

"You okay?"

"I'm fine!"

Keith smiled. "I can stop if you like."

Travis grunted. "No, don't stop. Fuck me."

Keith pulled out his fingers. The bright red head of his cock glowed almost purple. He put the modest head to Travis's tight hole and left it there, pressing very gently so the tip pushed forward a quarter of an inch every ten seconds.

Travis adjusted with each push until a minute passed. By then, the head was at the corona, which hurt like hell. Keith must have seen the pain on the boy's face.

He said, "This will make it better." He grabbed Travis by the waist and gave a hard shove, forcing the head past the boy's shitter.

A massive wave of relief swept through Travis's body. With the head past, Keith's shaft was a break from the pain. He felt the head moving deeper, stroking the button, and then deeper until it hit a wall at the end of his hole. Keith was buried all the way. It was a perfect fit.

"You ready to go to heaven?"

Travis nodded.

Keith said, "Here we go." He thrust and pulled, sliding the fat head of his cock over the joy buzzer. Travis twitched and writhed, overcome with pleasure. He couldn't believe his ass could make him feel so good. His little cock pulsed and spat out a gob of cum. He hadn't even touched it.

Keith whistled. "I wish my girlfriend came as easily as you!"

Travis wondered if Keith's girlfriend knew he did it with guys. But he stopped thinking and started feeling something new inside. The repeated strokes across that joy buzzer had caused something new to build inside him. It was like he was about to take a huge shit, but nothing was there. Then his insides quivered and spasmed. He bucked and thrashed in ecstasy. His ass muscles stroked Keith's cock.

Keith said, "Holy shit, keep doing that! Oh shit, I'm gonna..."

And the redhead released an explosive round of cum in Travis's ass. Travis became so turned on he shot another load into the air, spraying the bed, his chest, and Keith's face. His cum was everywhere.

"Damn, kid, where do you keep it?"

Travis blushed, ashamed of his little balls. Keith bent forward and kissed his lips. Their eyes met. "I'm sorry; I didn't mean that in a bad way. You're a little sperm factory. It means you liked what I was doing, and that's the best compliment."

Travis smiled. "It felt fucking great."

Keith pulled out, releasing a small flood of sperm that soiled his bedspread. "You made me cum harder than anyone before. You're a natural. A perfect bottom."

Travis wasn't expecting a compliment. He was so small, and all the guys in the porno magazines were so big. He said, "Keith, I'm too little. Why do you like doing it with me? Don't you like big ones?"

Keith shrugged. "I don't care if they're big or small, as long as the ass is big and tight. Your ass is fuckin' beautiful." He swatted Travis on the bottom and hitched up his pants.

"Get dressed. The guys won't notice we've been missing if we hurry. Come down a minute or two after me. I don't want them gossiping."

❧ 4 ❧

TRAVIS STANDS UP FOR
HIMSELF

Travis took the stairs slowly and limped into the kitchen. French Fry put away the sandwich fixings and wiped the countertop. Petey and Mike took one look at Travis and turned to Keith.

Petey said, "Did you give him the Hoffman welcome?"

Keith shrugged. "I don't know what you mean."

The whole kitchen broke out laughing. Travis blushed.

Petey said, "Keith is always the first. It's a good idea, anyway. He's the best at breaking in the new guy."

Travis was confused. Weren't they all straight? What was this?

French Fry put a hand on Travis's backside. "He took your cherry, didn't he?"

Travis ran out of the room, laughter echoing in his ears. He ran up to the bedroom and hid under the covers. He felt like a whore. A male whore. He liked getting fucked, and he felt ashamed. A soft knock came at the door. It was French Fry.

"Hey, Travis. Can I come in?"

Travis wiped the tears and snot from his face and said, "Yeah."

French Fry sat on the edge of the bunk and put a comforting hand on Travis's shoulder.

"Kid, we didn't mean nothing by it. We're your brothers. You're one of us. Shep, the guy who left, was like you. He had a sweet ass, and he liked to use it. We all got off with him."

Travis was confused. "I don't understand. You don't think I'm some sick, perverted freak?"

French Fry shook his head. "On the contrary. You're in the club. We're all into it. The four of us don't like to take it up the ass, but we sure appreciate a guy who does."

"Even Mike?"

French Fry chuckled. "He's in a foul mood because Shep was the only bottom boy who could take him. He has to whack off until he finds someone else."

"What about his girlfriend?"

French Fry grew serious. "He could kill a woman with that thing. Nearly did. No, he's strictly for men."

"Has he fucked you?"

French Fry smiled. "First of all, he'd kill me, too. Second of all, I ain't like that. It don't feel good. But I can tell it feels good for you. Most guys with small ones like it; big guys like me don't. I ain't proved it scientifically, but I think that's just how nature made us."

Travis was even more confused. His parents didn't think there was anything natural about it at all. "But they call us names."

French Fry sighed. "The men who call us faggots are either jealous or afraid. They don't know what they're missing."

Travis felt a strange veil lifting from his mind. He'd been stewing in shame and secrecy for so long that he felt naked without it. He wasn't a freak.

"You're a big guy?"

French Fry chuckled. "Long and skinny, like me. Yep."

"Longer than Keith?"

"Twice as long, but about as thick."

Travis tilted his head. "So you only can go in like halfway, then?"

"Oh, wait until I show you that secret."

The fire bell rang, interrupting their conversation.

"Come on!"

The two men slid down the pole and hopped onto the newly polished truck. It was so bright Travis had to shield his eyes with his free hand. They left the station and headed up the hill towards Twin Peaks. There was a fire at the radio station near the top. When they arrived, the engine from Station 26, Twin Peaks, was already there, and the fire was just a smolder. The damage was minor, and nobody was hurt. The Disc Jockey was coughing into his coat sleeve, his face blackened with smoke, but he would survive.

An overweight young fireman with long lashes sidled up to where Travis stood beside Mike as they reattached the hose to the truck.

He lisped as he said, "Hey, Mike. Is this your new Nancy boy?"

Mike turned and growled. "Fuck off, Shep."

The stranger smiled and stood his ground. He turned to Travis. "Be careful; he nearly killed a woman."

Mike leaped forward to connect with Shep, but his punch went into the air. The young man backed away, cackling like a hen. He ran back to his team, who scolded him.

Mike said, "Before you ask a bunch of questions, that's Shep. We shared a room before he got reassigned to Twin Peaks. He's a fucking queer, and I can't stand him."

The word hung in the air, fouler than any smoke from the burnt vinyl records.

Travis turned beet red. It wasn't shame anymore; it was anger. He heard the words coming from his mouth before he could stop them. "I'm a fucking queer."

Mike stopped what he was doing. "Okay, I didn't mean it like that. I'm sorry. I should have said 'asshole.'"

There was an awkward silence, then they both laughed. Mike was handsome, but he was a god when he smiled like that. Travis had to look away.

❧

BACK AT THE FIREHOUSE, TRAVIS WAS ON KITCHEN duty with French Fry. They made a version of spaghetti that would have made his mother cry with shame. It was watery tomato sauce over spaghetti that had boiled to mush. They shook the green can of imitation cheese over it to soak up the moisture. They cut a loaf of Francisco Sourdough in half and spread crushed garlic and butter. It smelled good, but French Fry left it in too long, and it burnt, and not just on the edges. To make it halfway presentable, Travis had to scrape it with a butter knife.

At dinner, Travis spoke up.

"If you want, I can make my Mama's recipe next time."

The room fell silent. French Fry said, "What's wrong with mine?"

Travis looked around the room. Every eye was on him; no one offered any assistance. "Uh, well, it's good old-fashioned American Spaghetti. You need to try real Italian, that's all."

Keith said, "Thank God somebody finally said something." They roared with laughter.

French Fry washed dishes while Travis dried them. They got into a rhythm, and soon the kitchen was spotless.

French Fry said, "Before the bell, you remember what we were talking about?"

Travis nodded.

"Yeah, well, I'd like to show you that secret tonight."

"But won't Keith mind?"

"He ain't got the exclusive, dude. I can switch with Petey tonight. He'll give me his single if I blow him."

5

FRENCH FRY SHOWS HIM
THE ROPES

Travis met up with French Fry in the hallway. "It's all set." He wiped his mouth. Petey left his room, whistling a happy tune.

"Have fun, boys. I already did."

French Fry adjusted his jaw. "Blowing that man is hard work. He's so fucking thick." He picked a hair out from between his teeth.

French Fry ushered Travis into the single room. It was nicer than the doubles. Instead of a bare bulb, it had a proper light with a cover. The bed was a double, with more room for the two men. French Fry unbuttoned Travis's pants. "Let me see."

Travis swatted at his hands involuntarily. "Uh, wait."

"I like the little ones, don't worry." Travis relaxed and let French Fry unbutton his pants. They fell to the floor, revealing his tiny penis and itty-bitty balls.

"Oh shit, that's hot." French Fry gripped his left thigh, squeezing his cock through his pants. "I gotta get these off before it gets stuck."

He dropped his pants, allowing his long, narrow cock to spring to attention. It was thicker than Keith's, but it was just an illusion; it looked thinner because it was so long.

French Fry said, "I wanna suck on that for a while. May I?"

Travis couldn't imagine why anyone would want to put such a little dick in their mouth, but he nodded his assent.

French Fry knelt, covering Travis's cock and balls with his mouth. He sucked and licked, sending shivers of delight through Travis. His knees buckled. French Fry pushed him so that he sat on the bed.

Clamped like a lamprey to Travis's crotch, French Fry tickled the tiny penis and balls. He let go long enough to say, "Oh fuck, it's better than eating pussy."

Travis could feel his cock leaking precum. It sent the tall man into a frenzy. He twisted the tiny genitals on his tongue, tickling them until, at last, Travis could hold back no longer.

"Fuck it; I'm gonna cum."

French Fry nodded. Travis felt his head grow light. His legs shook, and his hips bucked. He shot so much cum, it overflowed and ran down French Fry's chin.

French Fry held what he could in his mouth, then clamped onto Travis's asshole. He released the cum, letting it slip and slide up Travis's chute, making it warm and slippery.

French Fry stood, stroking his incredibly long cock. It was not too far from his knees when he pushed it down. He spat in his hand several times and slicked it up.

The head was narrow like the rest of his cock. He slipped it past Travis's hole without protest and slid up the chute until he hit the rear wall. Travis gasped, but he was surprised at how little it hurt.

"Ready for the secret?"

Travis nodded.

French Fry lifted Travis's right hip and thrust forward. With a loud 'pop,' the head pushed past the rectum.

Travis shrieked in astonishment. "What the fuck? Did you poke a hole in me?"

French Fry giggled. "I poked your hole, silly. That's your colon. Keith could never in a million years show you this little trick."

He pushed forward another four inches until he was all the way inside. Travis felt a sense of fullness, unlike anything he'd ever experienced.

French Fry liked to narrate. "Okay, I'm gonna pull back and forth past that hole, yeah? It feels good for me, but it's gonna feel fucking amazing for you. Are you ready?"

Travis said, "Fuck me."

In long, solid strokes, French Fry retreated from the colon then rushed back in, each time making the popping noise that sounded almost like a hand clap. Travis thought Keith's head rubbing against the joy buzzer was the best possible feeling on earth, but this topped it. His teeth chattered.

French Fry said, "That's how you know it's good. When you shiver like that."

Travis spasmed, shivered, chattered, and groaned. The muscle contractions in his ass spread to his colon. He was stroking French Fry with his insides.

"Holy Shit! I only ever heard about this, Travis. You can orgasm in your ass!"

Travis said nothing. He was past the point where words worked anymore. He howled like a cat in heat. French Fry echoed the sound in an ecstasy all his own as Travis's guts churned around his cock.

French Fry picked the boy up and carried him to the dresser, where he set him down. He was so tall; it was the perfect height for him to penetrate the boy completely. He picked up the pace until the clapping became applause.

Travis leaned back, lightheaded, and opened his mouth. French Fry kissed him, breathing life into him.

The connection was complete. Cock to ass to mouth to mouth. Like an electric train, the circuit between the two men flowed in a circle, then reversed, all the while powering French Fry's hips to pound at an ever-increasing pace.

Travis felt his legs wrap around his partner, pulling him closer. Then the orgasm coursing through his innards detoured to his loins. He shook violently.

Travis said, "I'm gonna cum."

"Me, too."

At the same instant, both men released a hot rush of semen. Travis's cum gushed up between the two men, soaking their chests and groin. French Fry blew his load deep inside Travis, in the middle of his sigmoid colon. He collapsed against the boy, gasping in deep breaths.

French Fry said, "I see we both had secrets to share."

Travis said, "Mine was a surprise for both of us."

French Fry backed up one step, then two, until, at last, the incredibly long, thin cock fell between his knees. Travis held his hand to catch the river of cum that followed. French Fry knelt and lapped it up.

"I love the taste of my cum when it's been in another man's ass."

Travis said, "It does taste good," as he licked his fingers clean.

French Fry sniffed the air. He looked down. "Gotta wash."

Travis was mortified. His poop was on the end of French Fry's cock.

"I-I'm so sorry."

French Fry laughed. "Us big guys are used to it. It comes with the territory." He retreated to the bathroom and washed his long dong in the sink.

The alarm didn't sound all night as the two men slept in each others' arms.

A RUDE ALARM WOKE THE TWO MEN. THEY DRESSED and slid down the pole, clinging to the side of the engine as it pulled out of the station. They rushed downhill to a bar in the Castro that was in flames. Fire Marshall Jordan was already on the scene.

He said, "Disgraceful. Arson. Mission Station put the fire out, but we need your help with the embers."

Travis ended up paired with Mike, his roommate. Mike grunted and rolled his eyes. Travis wasn't a nincompoop, but Mike had already made up his mind about him. Mike didn't trust Travis to do a good job.

Travis quickly grabbed the hose and ran it to the hydrant. Mike was hot on his heels, trying to wrench the hose from him so he could attach it.

"Hey, Mike, knock it off! I got it."

Mike growled. "It's nothing personal, T, you just don't do it right or fast enough!"

Travis said, "I'd be done by now if you'd just fucking let go!"

Mike dropped the hose and stormed off. Travis had it attached in fifteen seconds and turned the stem nut. Mike was astonished when he picked up the hose handle, and within seconds it spewed water at full flow. The hose nearly leaped out of his hands.

Travis sidled up to Mike, who aimed the hose onto the roof of the bar called "Toad Hall."

"Is it totaled?"

Mike shook his head - nah. Plenty of water damage, but the structure's still good. By the way, sorry I snapped at you just then. You did great."

Travis had no name for the rush of warm happiness that flooded his brain. Why did it matter if Mike was friendly to him?

The fire truck headed back up the hill, carrying the weary firemen to their beds. Everyone returned to their own bunks, so Travis and French Fry didn't get to continue their cuddle. The boy was so tired he just crashed in his bunk without a shower. Travis watched with one eye open as his roommate undressed and walked out to the hall with nothing but a towel slung over one shoulder. Envy crept into his soul as he watched the surreal meat bounce from one knee to another. He tried to stay awake to see Mike come back in, all wet from the shower, but sleep won.

The following day, the guys discussed the previous night's fire over scrambled eggs, toast, and coffee.

French Fry said, "Toad Hall was one of the best. I hope they catch the motherfucker."

Keith asked, "Do you think it was the owner trying to collect on his insurance?"

French Fry replied, "Are you nuts? That place was packed every night of the week! I got more tail there than Collingwood Park."

Petey smiled. "You guys were brave going there. We could lose our jobs just for hanging out at a fag bar."

Keith said, "Not all of us are in the closet, Petey. We got assigned to this station because they already knew one way or another. What about you, Travis? Do you go to the bars on Castro?"

Travis choked on his eggs. "I don't go there, no. If my folks found out, they'd kill me. Besides, I ain't old enough."

French Fry said, "They would let in a pretty boy like you, no question. The ABC be damned."

"What's the ABC?"

Mike answered. "It's a bunch of fucking fascists. The Alcoholic Beverage Commission. And they target the gay bars, trying to shut them down. If they find a minor in one of the bars, the place doesn't just get cited. They get their license suspended."

Keith added, "Meanwhile, the joints on Broadway

fill up with sixteen-year-old girls, and nobody cares. The ABC won't touch them."

Travis shrugged, "I guess they deserve it."

An audible hush fell over the room. Mike broke the silence. "Travis, you know you're one of us, right? None of us deserve harassment. Not even a little bitch like you."

The men laughed.

Petey put a reassuring hand on Travis's shoulder. He felt like a kind uncle. "Son, you're still learning who you are. Don't worry; we'll school you good."

French Fry said, "Teach you well, you dropout."

Petey smiled at the insult. He gestured to his crotch. "I got plenty of brains down here where it counts."

Travis quickly looked at the older man's bulge for the first time. It was pretty large so that the buttons of his jeans stretched the fabric.

Petey saw the glance. "Yep, it's big."

French Fry laughed. "You're not that long, and you know it."

Petey frowned. "Length don't mean much if you're thin as a pencil."

French Fry said, "I'd take my length any day over that fat motherfucking stump."

Petey ignored the insult and smiled at Travis. "My cock is average length but big as a can of beer. It's not for beginners."

Travis was curious. "I haven't seen a lot of dicks. What does it look like?"

Petey's smile turned into a mischievous grin. "I'll show you any time you're ready."

There were still a few hours until the shift ended. Travis couldn't get the picture out of his mind. A cock that thick would hurt like hell. But Travis wanted to see it, at least. His wish came true an hour later.

Travis had bathroom duty. He scrubbed the filthy

toilet, mopped the floors, and polished the faucets on the sink until they shone. He felt a pair of hands on his butt when he bent to put away the mop bucket.

"Sweet, they weren't lying."

Travis looked over his shoulder. It was Petey. A thrill ran through him.

"You ready to see it?"

Travis nodded.

Petey said, "Okay, but you gotta let me try to fuck you."

Travis locked the bathroom door. Petey's crotch had swollen to a monstrous bulge. Each button made an audible 'whoosh' when Petey unfastened it. He lowered the jeans, revealing a very full pair of Fruit of the Looms. The older man's cock stood out like a tent with a very thick pole.

"Go on, boy, pull them down."

Travis knelt in front of the grey-haired daddy and tugged on the waistband. He had to pull at an angle to release the monstrous thick cock, which slapped his chin when it finally escaped the fabric.

Travis backed away, scrambling like a frightened spider. "Holy shit!"

Petey laughed and started to put it away. The sheer volume of such a thick cock was unnerving. "Don't worry, Travis. I don't get much tail. All the boys are afraid of it."

Travis felt bad. "I promised."

Petey waved a hand in the air. "I was playing a joke."

Travis felt a strong urge to satisfy this man. "I'm not joking. I wanna at least try."

Petey's eyes lit up for a split second, then returned to the sad sparkle of a man accustomed to rejection. "You were a virgin a few days ago. I don't even want to try."

Travis pulled Petey's cock out of his hand and put it in his mouth. He could only lick the head; he watched as it swelled even further so that he needed a second hand to stroke it.

Petey sighed. "Okay, let's get this over with." Travis bent over the sink. The older fireman reached under the sink and pulled out a can of Crisco. "This works best."

The foxy daddy put a wide finger into the tub of shortening and wiped it on Travis's asshole. He gently inserted the finger. Travis wriggled with delight.

"Let me know when you're ready for another finger."

Travis stretched his cheeks in response. Petey raised an eyebrow and put another finger in the boy's young hole.

He said, "Oh fuck, you're a pussy boy."

Travis turned to look over his shoulder with a frown. "Hey!"

Petey waved a hand. "It's not an insult. I meant you got an ass made for dick, like a pussy. It's a rare find. Be proud."

Travis felt a flood of warmth, receiving praise from this seasoned fireman. The approval made him horny. He rode back and forth on Petey's two fingers, sliding down to the knuckles.

"Keep going."

Petey put a third, then a fourth finger into the boy's widening hole. "Holy shit, boy, you're a quick study."

Travis beamed with pride. When Petey added in his thumb, Travis rode all five digits and pressed against the knuckles. In one sharp move, he impaled himself, and Petey slid in up to the wrist. The pain was intense for a second, but it felt great once he passed the fist.

Petey whistled. "Oh man, I think I'm gonna do this."

He punched the boy's ass, withdrawing and pushing his hand in until the hole stayed open for a second before clapping shut.

Petey stroked his cock with one hand and rubbed Travis's tiny penis with the other. Travis got wet right away. He felt pressure on his hole, then blinding pain as Petey pushed the head into his hole. It was no thicker than his fist, but there was no wrist. The cock was the same width as the head, and there was no relief as the corona pushed its way into his shitter.

Travis whimpered. "Back it up for a sec."

Petey sighed. "I knew it."

Travis said, "No, just hold it right there for a bit." Petey was most of the way out so that the tip was stretching the boy's hole, but not completely.

"Okay." Travis pushed towards Petey, and the head slipped back in.

Petey exhaled in a shaky breath. "Oh god, that feels so good."

Travis said, "Fuck me."

The older man needed no more encouragement. He sawed back and forth, pulling out entirely before plunging back in. The shape of his cock made it easy for him to go all the way. Travis felt his pubes tickle his bottom on the instroke.

"Oh damn, that's sweet." Petey was in bliss, but so was Travis. The thick cock milked his prostate. Long webs of sticky pre-cum dribbled from his hard little penis and stretched to the floor. Petey scooped it up and licked it.

"You taste better than pussy."

Travis said, "I want to see your face."

He turned over so he was on his back, then nodded. As Petey pushed back in, the boy wrapped his legs around his waist, pulling him close, then releasing and letting him pull out.

Air built up in Travis's ass, and he tried to hold it in, but his hole was gaping, and it escaped with a soft roar.

Petey threw his head back, beads of sweat flying

through the air. "That sound, I haven't heard it in years."

Travis played with the man's nipples through his t-shirt.

"Yeah, pinch those titties, boy." Petey stripped the shirt off. His nipples were thick like his cock. They stuck out like two gumdrops on his chest. Travis was fascinated. He'd never seen such big nipples. He twisted them gently between his fingers.

"Harder!" As Petey commanded the boy to torture his tits, he picked up the pace of his fucking. Travis grunted but never stopped smiling. He knew if he showed too much pain, the man would stop pounding his hole.

With both hands on the man's thick nipples, Travis felt an energy surge between the men. Their eyes locked. Without warning, Travis's tiny penis unleashed several thick ropes of cum. It landed on his face and chest.

"Did I do that?" Petey was astonished.

Travis nodded. "Keep going; I can do it again."

Petey's ass was a blur as he fucked hard; Travis couldn't hold back a moan.

"Am I hurting you?"

He was, but Travis shook his head. The pain paled in comparison to the pleasure. "Keep. Going. Petey." His words came out in between the sound of Petey's hips smacking into his bottom. There was a knock on the door.

"Hey, some of us gotta take a shit!"

Petey was close. "You ready for it?"

Travis shook his head. "Hold it in until I cum again."

"Hurry up."

The boy touched himself and rubbed like a woman playing with her clit. He felt a building wave of ecstasy, but because it was his second time coming, the pleasure didn't increase as quickly. He was building towards a slow orgasm. Suddenly, his ass began to spasm.

"Oh shit, Pete, I'm close."

"Yeah, me too!"

Travis grunted, his ass stretched so wide he thought it would split him in two. Petey fucked faster and harder than any other guys he'd been with. Travis moaned and lay his head against the mirror above the sink.

Petey said, "I can't hold it anymore. Aaaargh!" Travis felt the man's cock swell even further. The pain won out over the pleasure, and Travis cried out. "Fuck! Fuck!" The pain served as a catalyst. Travis could feel the familiar peak of pleasure, then his cock spit out a massive second helping of cum, over and over.

"Oh god!" Petey was there. He stopped fucking and held the boy's ass against his thighs. A warm flood of daddy cum had nowhere to go but up Travis's bumhole and into the colon.

Another fist pounded on the door.

Petey kissed Travis on the lips. "Thank you." His voice cracked like he might cry. He was so grateful; it showed.

Travis winked. "Thank YOU, Petey."

They dressed and let French Fry in. He rushed past them and sat on the toilet. "Get the fuck out of here!"

That afternoon, Travis walked down the hill to his parent's house. Each step caused him pain. He couldn't walk right. To make matters worse, he farted cum in his jeans. Thankfully, he was wearing a long coat that hid the spreading stain. He wondered how his mother would react if she knew what it was.

6

MEET THE TURK

When Travis arrived at the firehouse for his next shift, he was the first to get there. A man with a Turkish mustache opened the door. His t-shirt was straining against his broad, muscular chest. He was so hairy that a few stray hairs poked through the fabric.

"You the new guy?"

Travis nodded.

The man extended his hand. "Turk."

Travis's eyes strayed down to the man's crotch. It looked full.

"Whatcha lookin' at, faggot?"

Travis gulped. "Sorry, I like your shoes."

The man smirked. "They're plain leather boots from Sears. You weren't looking at 'em." He adjusted his crotch.

Travis smiled weakly. "You're just so...big."

The man gave a nasty grin. "Damn right." He adjusted his crotch again, revealing a thick cock pressed against his thigh.

"You're on the faggot shift; I ain't stupid. You were looking at it." Turk bristled with anger. "It's strictly for mouth and pussy. Women."

Travis tried to make conversation. "Are you married?"

"Hell no! I play the field, son."

Travis glanced down again. He couldn't help it. "I'll bet the ladies love you."

Turk wasn't immune to a compliment. "Yeah, I'm pretty popular. I always make 'em come, so they can't get enough of it." He stroked his cock through his jeans. "It's almost too big for them to suck. Women don't know how to suck dick."

Travis wasn't sure he heard right. "They don't? How do you know."

Turk sized the boy up. "I like a good blow job. A good one, though. A mouth is a mouth."

Travis recalled his tryst with the stranger in the bookstore. He made the guy come, so he knew he was pretty good at it. The memory made him lick his lips.

Turk put a firm hand on Travis's shoulder. "Come on; I'll let you suck it."

They went upstairs to the bathroom. Turk locked the door and shoved Travis roughly to his knees. "You better not give me any teeth, son."

Travis shook his head. "No, sir. I won't."

Turk lowered his zipper and reached into his jeans. He hauled out a big, soft cock. It looked like it was five inches long. "Get it hard."

Travis put the soft cock in his mouth and swallowed until it was at the back of his throat. It began to swell as Turk whispered. "Yeah, boy, you like that big dick, right?"

Travis nodded and sucked on the man's meat, which was growing and thickening even more. Soon he had to stretch his mouth to avoid his teeth grazing the flesh.

"Oh fuck, you're good."

Travis didn't know what made him good, but he appreciated the compliment. The cock had grown at least three inches. He had to swallow it down his throat to get to the base, so he did.

"Oh shit, how the fuck do you faggots do that?" Turk pinched a nipple through his t-shirt. "That feels so fucking good."

Travis used his tonsils to stroke the head of Turk's cock. He gagged a few times, but he was able to control it. A thick saliva gathered in his mouth, making the cock extra slippery. It slid down his throat easily.

Turk's breath grew shallow as he swelled to full size. It was so thick that it hurt Travis's jaw. But the boy was determined to give the man the best head of his life, so he stretched like a snake to keep his teeth off the big, beautiful cock in his mouth. He pulled back and took a long breath.

"Don't stop!" Turk growled roughly and held Travis by the ears, fucking his face. He forced his fat cock down Travis's throat and groaned. "Fuck! Why can't women do it like this?"

Turk leaned against the sink, his muscular butt pressing against Travis's fingers. Travis pulled his hands out before The hairy beast crushed them.

"Shit, sorry, man."

Travis shrugged and kept sucking. Turk wrapped his big hands around Travis's head and shoved hard. Travis couldn't breathe, and he patted Turk's thigh. Turk fucked deep, not caring that the boy was choking. With his big butt against the sink, Travis couldn't push away. He panicked. At last, Turk let go, and Travis pulled back, gasping. He barely caught his breath before Turk pushed him back down.

"I'm gonna come, and you better fuckin' swallow it."

Travis nodded and let Turk use him like the sex dolls with open mouths he'd seen in the bookstore.

Turk licked his mustache and grunted. "Fuck, here it comes!" With his cock lodged in Travis's esophagus, he fed the boy a large volume of cum. Travis didn't need to swallow - it went right down the chute. He needed air, but the airway was still blocked by Turk's long, fat cock. He felt faint.

"Mmph!" Travis smacked Turk's thigh, trying to get him to back off.

"You'll get air when I'm good and ready." He was still spurting in smaller and smaller amounts. Travis broke free and came off the cock, getting the last load on his face.

"You fucking bitch, I wasn't ready." Turk slapped Travis and laughed. "It's okay. That was the best fucking blowjob of my life, right until the last moment, anyway." He threw a paper towel at Travis, zipped up, and left the boy kneeling on the bathroom floor to clean up.

7

TRAVIS PERFORMS
MIRACLES

Travis was hoarse over dinner.

"You're not getting sick, are you?" Petey looked concerned.

Travis said, "Nah, it's just a frog in my throat."

Keith said, "That's not what I heard from Turk." The men burst into laughter.

Travis blushed. "Everyone knows?"

Mike smiled. "He gave a glowing recommendation. Said you might even be able to handle me. That's a laugh. Nobody, especially you, could blow me."

Hearing that challenge, Travis decided he would prove Mike wrong if he ever got the chance.

There were no calls between dinner and bedtime. After watching Johnny Carson on the crappy black and white TV, the men filed upstairs to their beds. Mike took Travis aside.

"I'm sorry if I was mean at dinner."

Travis shrugged. "It wasn't mean. It was just wrong."

Mike frowned. "You've seen it; you know it doesn't fit in anyone's mouth. I've never had a blowjob in my life. It just doesn't happen."

Travis said, "I'll bet you I can."

Mike said, "You're on. But if you lose, I'm sticking it up your ass. I am sick and tired of jacking off."

Travis thought to himself that it was a win-win situation, but he wanted to give Mike his first blowjob. He was growing fond of his jerk of a roommate. He wanted to show him a good time.

Mike sat on the lower bunk, his legs wide. He waited for Travis to unzip him. He didn't wear underwear - there was no point. Nothing could contain a monster like Mike. Travis reached down the right pant leg, searching for the head of his cock. He was nearly to the knee when he found the soft, fleshy mushroom. He squeezed it and tried to pull it out. It wouldn't double over.

Mike said, "Nah, you gotta do it from up here." He put Travis's hand on the root of his massive cock. "You'll need to hurry because I'm getting hard."

Travis struggled to wrestle the cock out of his roommate's pants. It was so thick and getting thicker by the second.

Mike said, "Never mind, let me do it." He stood and slid his pants down slowly, revealing inch after inch of the humongous slab of meat. Mike smiled, watching Travis's eyes widen with each passing moment.

Travis gulped. He realized he was in for a lot of hard work whether he won the bet or not. That cock was beyond all imagination. And it was still growing.

Mike had to bend at the waist to get his pants past the tip. When they were below his knee, the colossal cock sprung to life, still only half-hard. When Mike sat back down, Travis grabbed it, hoping to get some of it in his mouth before it grew too big. He opened his mouth as wide as possible and put the tip in. To his surprise, he was able to get past the corona.

Mike whistled. "Shit, son. That's the first time anyone has...oh!"

Travis had somehow unhinged his jaw like a snake and ingested the massive log of flesh like a boa constrictor eating an elephant. It reached the back of his throat and caught on his tonsils.

"Oh fuck, Travis. That's fucking amazing."

Travis, whose throat was already sore from his earlier affair with Turk, felt a burning, tearing sensation as Mike moved past his tonsils and down his throat. His Adam's apple came forward as the massive cock went further down his throat. Mike, stunned beyond belief, lay back on the bed and groaned. Travis thought he heard sobs. Desperate for air, he pulled back and took a deep breath before pushing Mike deep into his throat again.

Mike spoke through tears. "I don't believe it. It's a fucking miracle."

Travis grunted his agreement. Nothing this big belongs in a human throat. Every nerve in his throat was screaming at him, but he kept at it, massaging the tip of his cock with his tonsils as it made the long journey down his throat and back again. His neck muscles spasmed, causing the esophagus to clamp down. It was a gag reflex, but there was no way anything was getting past Mike's enormous cock. The effect put Mike into a state of bliss. Travis involuntarily massaged the cock with his throat.

When he finally pulled up for air, a small amount of bile came out. Mike sat up.

"Hey, hey. You don't have to finish. You won." He stood up, and his massive meat crashed to his knees. Travis stood up. Mike hugged him tight. "You won, little buddy. You don't have to take me up your ass tonight."

Travis said, "But I want to. I want you inside me."

Mike kicked off his shoes and stepped out of his pants. "Well, alright then." He crawled into the bunk with his back against the wall. His cock stretched out across the narrow mattress and hung in the air, throbbing. "I don't know how you'll do it, but come to bed."

Travis removed his clothes, revealing the miniature penis that sprouted from his pubic mound. Mike whistled appreciatively. "That is such a beautiful little dick. I love it."

Travis was pleased that Mike liked his tiny dick.

Mike said, "You know where I keep the Vaseline. Can you hand it to me?"

Travis obeyed. Mike took a generous amount on his fingers and rubbed it up and down the length of his cock, dipping back in for refills several times. "Come here." He pulled Travis by the waist and rubbed his goopy fingers on Travis's hole, putting one, then two, inside the boy.

Mike said, "It's okay if you can't handle it. You already made me the happiest man in Eureka Valley."

Travis smiled. He held the head to his hole. Mike was no thicker than Petey, so the struggle was less than Mike expected. After three tries, the tip was inside. Mike got wider in the middle. Travis pushed through the pain until enough of Mike was inside him, and he could lie on the edge of the bed. He pushed until the fat cock got stuck at the end of his rectum.

Mike pulled back and started humping, holding Travis by the waist to keep him from falling off the edge of the bed.

"That's good. Just hold still and let me do the work."

But Travis wasn't done. He lifted his leg and rotated his waist so that Mike's cock was hitting the junction to the sigmoid colon, and the tip pushed against the valve. With each rough thrust, the valve loosened until, suddenly, the head popped past with a loud snap.

Mike freaked out. "Oh shit, little buddy, did I hurt you?"

Travis shook his head, pushing his ass closer and closer to Mike, letting the incredible cock fill his colon.

Mike was astonished. "How are you doing that."

Travis reached back and put a finger to Mike's lips. "Just enjoy it. Don't speak."

Every nerve in Travis's body screamed against the invasion of his insides, but he ignored it. The desire to please Mike, to really give him something good, was far more important than any pain.

Mike was too happy to stay quiet. "I can't fucking believe it. How are you doing that?"

In response, Travis thrust his hips toward Mike. The fireman held Travis close until his long, thick cock hit the magic button at the end of the sigmoid colon. Travis felt his insides kick into motion.

Mike said, "Oh fuck, I've never been so deep. And I've never felt anything like this."

Travis was at the edge of consciousness. Just a few days ago, he had been a virgin. Now he was stretched to his limits, nestled in the arms of his handsome roommate. He leaned his head back so it rested against Mike's chest. They fucked sideways for a few minutes. Every time Mike thrust, Travis pushed back to meet him, pressing that button at the end of his sigmoid colon. Mike began to take longer strokes, as much as the wall at his back would allow. This way, he could slip the softball-sized head in and out of the junction. Travis's whole body spasmed each time it passed the spot.

"Oo-oh-oh-oh," Travis had no words, just moans of ecstasy.

Mike said, "Christ, you're good. A natural. I've prayed for someone like you my whole life." He kissed Travis's neck, then nibbled his ear."

Travis hadn't known what he wanted before this, but he knew he'd found it. Words weren't possible, so he just nodded his head and reached back to stroke Mike's firm thighs and curvaceous buttocks.

When Mike touched Travis's little penis, it leaked

sticky fluid immediately. He said, "You got a wet little clit there, boy."

Travis wriggled in response, letting the pleasure of such intimate contact overwhelm his senses. He gushed pre-cum like it was a thin stream of urine. It stained the bedsheets and soiled Mike's hand. The older fireman licked his fingers clean.

"God, you taste good."

Travis managed a word. "Yeah."

Mike's fucking technique was slow, cautious, and deliberate. He had never met anyone with whom he could completely let go and fuck with wild abandon.

Travis said, "Harder."

Mike was astonished. He picked up the pace. Travis reached back and pushed his buttocks to encourage him to go faster and deeper. Mike realized he could speed things up, so he did.

"Is this alright?"

Travis was going to lose his ability to speak once more, so he croaked, "Harder."

Mike shrugged. He fucked with all his might. His cock protruded from Travis's belly, making it look like a circus tent collapsing and rebuilding repeatedly. He put his hand on the spot above Travis's navel where his monster cock protruded. Travis covered his big hands with his delicate fingers. He rubbed them hard, so Mike was rubbing his own cockhead through the thin layer of skin and bowel that sat between his cock and his hand. It was a strange sensation, and it pushed him closer to orgasm.

Travis rubbed Mike's rough hands, marveling at their size and strength. As he traced the knuckles, a familiar warm feeling rushed through his groin to his tiny dick. He was going to cum.

"Oh fuck, Mike. I'm—" It was too late. He splattered the edge of the bed and the floor with six or seven shots of sperm.

Mike said, "You didn't even touch yourself."

Travis nodded. "You did that."

Mike pounded the boy hard. He was close. "Oh fuck, that was so hot. Oh man, oh Travis, you're so fucking sexy."

Travis let the words wash over him like a warm shower. His grumpy hot roommate was into him. It was a dream come true.

Mike's strokes grew increasingly rapid until he was in a fucking frenzy.

"Here it comes! It's coming! It's coming. I'm gonna come. I—" he groaned loudly and held Travis tight to his waist. His thighs, covered in sweat, were slipping and sliding on the boy's backside. His groan dissolved into a sigh. He was so far inside the boy Travis could barely feel the release until it hit a nerve deep up inside. Like a fountain, Mike pumped stream after stream of warm cum into Travis. Mike held Travis tight, spooning with the boy, buried so deep inside him he couldn't pull out from his prone position. He pushed gently on Travis's back, but the boy shook his head.

"No, Mike, I want you inside me all night long."

Mike blushed. "I don't know how to sleep like this."

Travis said, "Try."

As Mike's cock shrank deep inside Travis, the cum leaked from the sides. He said, "Come on, let's wash up."

Travis sighed and gingerly put a leg on the floor to help him off the bed. He rolled and felt the soft log of flesh move through his guts until it popped past the junction and out his hole. It was followed by a torrent of cum splattering all over the floor.

The rest of the firehouse seemed to be sound asleep. The two lovers tiptoed to the shower, where they explored each other in the warm stream of water. Mike held up his cock head to Travis's penis. Just the head was longer than Travis's whole dick. He chuckled.

"Small guys like you are just as rare as big guys like me. It's hot."

Travis blushed. His mind was fixated on the Tom of Finland drawing with massive cocks everywhere. He knew he could never be in a drawing like that. But Mike was sincere. He rubbed his cockhead on Travis's crotch, teasing it until it got hard and stood out, maybe an inch and a half long.

Mike started to get hard again. "Hey, let's do it again."

Travis could feel his insides begging for a break, but his heart and mind wanted more closeness with this freak of a man.

"Whatever you want, Mike. I'm yours."

They pulled the bottom bunk mattress onto the floor, making it easier for them to get into new positions. Travis buried his face in the pillow with his loose, stretchy ass raised, and Mike fucked him like a dog. He rutted and thrust hard, hurting Travis, who said nothing. He was so happy to be Mike's sex object that it didn't matter.

When Mike came a second time, he pulled out fast. A trickle of blood came with the cum.

"We better stop for the night."

Travis said, "Okay, but I need you inside me when we sleep." Mike obliged. Travis snored lightly, his roommate buried deep in his hole. Mike soon followed him into the land of dreams.

8

STUFFING THE TURKEY

When the two men awoke, Mike was still inside. Travis stood slowly, letting the snake-like cock wriggle out of his ass. It hit the floor with a loud thud.

"Ow!" Mike held the head in his hands and rubbed it like a bumped knee.

Travis was horrified. "I'm so sorry, Mike."

Mike laughed. "It was more of a shock. It doesn't hurt. Hey, look at that. You got pussy lips!"

Travis examined his ass in the mirror. Sure enough, the edges were like flaps, grey and puckered. He had a pussy in his ass. He spread his cheeks and pushed. His hole gaped wide open, expelling a roar of air that had been trapped since the night before.

The two men had only slept a few hours. They shuffled down to breakfast. Travis walked with a limp. When he entered the kitchen, the other three firemen laughed.

"Travis get the ol' firehose?" Keith smiled broadly.

Mike nodded, glancing from face to face with a sly grin.

Petey said, "We broke him in. Is he better than Shep?"

Mike said, "Shep can't hold a candle to Travis." He put an arm around the boy.

French Fry said, "There's peace in the Middle East. Hallelujah!"

Mike said, "I wasn't that bad, was I?"

The table went silent. Mike laughed hard. "Okay, sorry, gentlemen. If Travis will have me, there will be peace."

Every eye turned to Travis, who blushed. He said, "I like it. A lot."

Petey whistled. "Hot damn! We got Mike back. Travis, you're a godsend."

French Fry said, "You willing to share him?"

Mike said, "Hell no! Get your own boy."

French Fry looked around the room. "I just see a bunch of top guys looking for a bottom."

Travis felt strange being discussed like the last piece of bacon at breakfast. He understood he was valuable, a hot commodity. But he was human, not an object or a piece of meat. He thought about it at the end of the shift as he limped down the hill to his parents.

His mother met him at the door. "Travis, what's wrong? You're walking with a terrible limp."

Travis wondered what would happen if he told the truth. He couldn't. "I slid down the pole too hard and hurt my leg. It's no big deal."

"Let me see that leg."

Travis gave an exhausted sigh. "I'm fine, ma! What's for dinner?"

She held a wooden spoon in one hand, dyed red with San Marzano tomato sauce. "Lasagna Bolognese."

Travis's face lit up. It was his favorite dish. His mother made it the old-world way, with layers of bechamel sauce and fresh mozzarella from Rossi's deli.

"You go sit in the living room, and I'll call you when it's ready."

"Where's Dad?"

She said, "He's napping. Be quiet, and don't bother him."

Travis couldn't sit on the sofa; it was too hard. He took his father's overstuffed recliner. When he leaned back and lifted the leg rest, it took some gravity off his puffy hole. The lips had swollen to the size of sausages. They were extremely tender. He was sleepy. His neck could barely hold his head, which lolled to one side.

He was awoken rudely by his father. "Travis, was ist das? That's my chair. Get up!"

"Sorry, Pa, I hurt my leg, and it felt better.

His father softened. "Okay, sorry. You rest up. That sofa is the devil's birth table. I'll get a chair from the kitchen.

Travis wondered idly why his family held on to such a useless piece of furniture. He figured it was expensive, and they were too proud to return it. Now it had been in the house for years. He vowed to use his next paycheck to get them an overstuffed sofa to match the recliner.

"La cena è pronta!" Mama called from the kitchen. When Travis sat gently at the table, he saw two full pans come out of the oven.

"Mama, we're never gonna eat all that!"

"No, I know, it's for your coworkers. I put this one in the fridge, and you bring it next time you work."

When two days passed, Travis took the lasagna pan, wrapped in aluminum foil, up the hill to the station. Petey greeted him.

"What's this?"

"Mama's lasagne. You don't have to eat it if you don't want to."

Petey lifted a corner and sniffed. "Holy shit, that smells good. Are you kidding? We'll have a feast! I'll make a salad and garlic bread. It'll be perfect."

When supper rolled around, the men came into the

kitchen early, one by one, sniffing the air. "What is that? It smells fucking delicious!"

They sat down to the best lasagne of their lives. It had none of that awful San Francisco ricotta cheese, which made lasagne slimy. It was rich, chewy, cheesy, and meaty.

Mike looked at Travis in a new way. "Did you make this?"

Travis said, "It was my mama, but I know how."

French Fry said, "I nominate you as head chef."

Travis liked cooking, especially for these guys. His mama could help prep the ingredients so he wouldn't be stuck in the kitchen the whole day. He thought of his specialties - Veal Scallopine, Chicken Cacciatore, Eggplant Parmigiana, Cannelloni; it would be easy to make these men happy. Making Mike happy that night was hard work.

After a false alarm, a burnt turkey in the oven of a junkie who nodded out, the men returned to the firehouse laughing.

"French Fry, that guy's turkey was better than yours!"

"Shut Up! It wasn't burnt."

"It was undercooked, which is worse."

Mike caught Travis's eye and smiled wide. The older man whispered, "I'll be stuffing your turkey tonight. Both ends."

Travis's jaw still hurt from the last time. But he was determined to keep Mike happy. He was feeling increasingly fond of his roommate. He was like a Tom of Finland drawing come to life. Travis didn't know how he fit into the picture but knew he belonged to Mike. Being owned was equally disturbing and thrilling. They pulled both mattresses on the floor at bedtime to increase the potential for new positions. Travis knelt on the edge of the mattress; Mike stood with his hands on his hips, his big dick swinging like a flesh pendulum. Travis swooped and caught it in his mouth, swallowing it like a baby bird with a massive worm. It grew quickly, stretching his mouth and filling it with throbbing flesh.

Mike let out a loud, contented sigh. Travis gobbled the cock down, letting it stretch and swell in his throat until his Adam's apple drew tight on his neck. The head got lodged so tightly that Travis couldn't pull back. He panicked, flailing at Mike's leg to let him know. Mike's eyes were closed, and he still stood too far from Travis for his arms to reach. Travis couldn't get any air to make a noise. He smacked Mike's cock hard.

"Ow! What the hell?" His anger quickly dissolved to fear. Travis was turning blue, and Mike was jammed in his throat. He stepped backward, dragging Travis off the edge of the mattress. Travis flailed his arms. He couldn't get any traction on the hard linoleum floor.

Mike put a foot on Travis's shoulder as leverage and tugged on his cock until it finally dislodged with a loud pop. Mike staggered backward as Travis fell to the floor, gasping like a landed fish.

Mike pulled up his pants, grabbing his cock, ready to shove it down the pant leg.

Travis gasped, "Wait, No!"

Mike stopped. "I nearly fucking killed you. How can I get hard if I'm worried about murder?"

Travis thought fast. He rolled back onto the mattress, knees by his ears, and spread his butt cheeks. He flexed his ass muscles, creating a gaping hole. "Don't you want this?"

Mike licked his lips. The boy's hole was a small, dark cave. He wanted to put his cock in there. He felt himself swell in response.

Travis was prepared. He grabbed a big gob of Vaseline and spread it up and down Mike's hardening pipe. It throbbed in response to his touch. He wiped the remainder inside his hole. He took the head and put it right where it belonged, at the entry to his flesh cave.

Mike needed no further encouragement. He pushed in as he lowered his knees to the mattress. His cock bumped into the familiar place where Travis's rectum ended. He gently lifted Travis's hip and slipped past the junction. He walked on his knees until Travis was packed, and his pubic bush tickled the boy's bottom.

"Fuck me." Travis wriggled with anticipation.

Like a locomotive leaving the station, Mike gathered speed as he sawed back and forth in long strokes. He massaged his cockhead by dragging it back and forth through the tight colo-rectal valve. As Mike accelerated, Travis grabbed the edges of the mattress and thrashed.

Mike asked, "Am I hurting you?"

Travis shook his head hard. "Oh god, Mike. Please don't stop!"

The big fireman continued his invasion of Travis's colon. The clapping sound was loud and satisfying. Travis felt warm vibrations course through his lower body and then went into a spasm of pleasure.

Mike whistled. "I'll never get tired of it when you do that."

Travis spoke between gritted teeth. "It's not me; it's my body. You make me do that."

That made Mike swell with pride, both in his chest and his cock. He watched in awe as his thick cock stretched the slender boy's belly, protruding in that same spot above the navel. Travis followed Mike's eyes and caught the lump in his hands, massaging it through his belly skin. Mike went wild, pounding hard. Travis moaned at the intoxicating blend of pleasure and pain coursing through him. The spasms continued. Then the fire station bell sounded.

Mike pulled out fast. Travis doubled over with a painful cramp when his insides snapped shut. He struggled to his feet. Mike was already in his jeans and pulling up his bunker pants. Travis moved slowly, his insides still punishing him for taking such a huge cock.

Fully dressed, the men slid down the pole and leaped onto the truck. Petey shared the details. A four-unit apartment on 17th and Sanchez was burning out of control. They were the first fire truck on the scene. Travis hooked the hose to the hydrant and nodded at Mike, who signaled it was time to turn the nut. Once the water was flowing, Travis saw the residents outside. One woman was screaming. The fire had trapped her baby in the second-floor apartment. French Fry ran into the building with his equipment and emerged holding the screaming infant. The mother collapsed in tears, rocking her baby.

On the ride back to the station, Mike stood close to Travis. He put a meaty hand down Travis's pants and fingered his loose hole, still greasy with Vaseline. Travis leaned back, feeling Mike's breath on his neck.

"I want to fuck your hole so bad." He said it in a hoarse whisper.

Travis said, "Good."

While Petey, Keith, and French Fry showered, Travis and Mike got back to business.

Mike slipped back in smoothly. When Travis wrapped his legs around Mike's waist, the strong firefighter picked him up and carried him around the room. Travis bounced up and down on the huge pole.

Mike said, "Oh, fuck yeah, keep doing that."

Travis rode Mike's cock, milking it with his insides. Mike set him down on the dresser. He pounded hard, knocking the dresser into the wall repeatedly.

Travis didn't care if the whole firehouse knew what they were doing. They'd done it to him already, only not as well. Mike had found the perfect hole. Travis looked into Mike's eyes. He looked away. Travis leaned forward until his lips touched Mike's. Mike put a hand on Travis's chest as if to push him away, but he didn't.

Travis caressed Mike's mouth with his own, then they kissed. Electromagnetic energy surged through their bodies. Mike's hand moved from Travis's chest to his nipple. He pinched the flesh between his enormous thumb and forefinger. Travis squirmed, kissing harder. The energy surged like a burst of static electricity. The two men jumped and laughed, then kissed some more. The tingle following the shock persisted like a gentle current.

Mike picked Travis off the dresser, then twirled him until he faced away. Travis's feet touched the ground. Travis put his arms forward and braced himself against the wall. Mike pummeled his insides, causing his knees to shake and bend. Mike held the young man's waist to keep him steady. His long strokes slowed slightly, signaling he was getting closer to orgasm.

Just thinking about Mike coming inside, Travis got too excited and, without touching himself, shot his load on the floor. Mike saw the boy's spunk and lost control. He pounded harder and faster than he'd ever dreamed he could. Travis whined and whimpered with joy and pain.

"Fuck me, Mike. Oh fuck! Just like that! Right there! Right there!"

Mike roared. "Fuck! Here it comes!" He pulled Travis's hips and held himself all the way inside. Travis could feel the cock moving of its own volition as it churned out ounce after ounce of warm cum inside him. Mike rubbed his stubble on Travis's shoulder. Travis turned, and their lips met in another electrified kiss. Neither man had felt that energy before, but they knew it was love.

❅ 9 ❅
NICK'S COVE

At breakfast, there were snickers and comments around the breakfast gossip table. Neither Travis nor Mike were bothered by the jokes, innuendoes, and jeers. They quietly ate and gazed into each other's eyes, oblivious to any comments. The other men realized their taunts were falling on deaf ears and stopped.

Keith said, "I don't think we're gonna get to pass Travis around anymore."

Mike rubbed a crumb from Travis's mouth. Travis blushed and looked at the floor.

French Fry clapped the air. "Hey, Earth to Mike! Are you there?"

Mike came out of his reverie and glanced at his coworkers. "Sorry, guys. What were you saying?"

The men laughed. Keith whacked Mike on the shoulder. "I'm glad you found something good. Gives the rest of us hope."

Mike smiled, then looked at Travis. "You'd better not break my heart, kid. I'll die."

Travis nodded. The other three firefighters said, "Awwww! Mike and Travis, sitting in a tree, K-I-S-S-I-N-G!"

Mike said, "What are you, frickin' kindergartners?"

After breakfast, Mike asked Travis if he wanted to come stay with him at his Tenderloin studio.

"I gotta ask my parents first. Would you like to come over for lunch? Mom will be cooking something good."

Mike said, "Isn't it too early to meet your folks?"

Travis shrugged. "They don't know about me. Just keep it cool, and you'll get the best meal of your life."

The two men walked down the hill to Travis's home. He opened the door and yelled, "Hey, ma! I brought a friend. We got enough?"

His mother stepped into the hallway, wiping her floury hands on her apron. "I made Pasta Fazool. Does your friend like beans?"

The hunky fireman extended a hand, "I'm Mike."

Travis's mother blushed. She shook the air. "I got pasta dough all over my hands. It's nice to meet you. I'm Maria. Such a handsome man!"

Mike grinned. When she returned to the kitchen, he said, "Your mom's got good taste. Like mother, like son." Travis whacked Mike's arm.

"Where's Papa?"

"Here I am!" Travis's father came down the stairs, eyeing Mike warily. "Who's this?"

Mike shook the man's hand. "I'm Mike, sir. I work with your son."

"I'm Fritz. What are you doing here?"

Travis snapped, "He's having lunch with us."

Maybe his father could see the electricity between the two men, or perhaps he just didn't like strangers in his house. Either way, he wasn't very friendly to the visitor.

When Mike took his first bite of the bean and pasta soup, his eyes widened. "This is so fu— darn good!"

Fritz snorted. "It's not her best." He excused himself, throwing his napkin on the table.

Mike said, "I don't think your dad likes me."

Maria said, "Don't mind him. He's in pain. Arthritis makes him like that."

Travis said, "Ma, you know it's not that. He's a dick."

"Language!" Maria pounded the table. "Sorry, Mike, you shouldn't have to watch our family fighting."

Mike shrugged. "Feels just like home."

Maria chuckled. "I like this one, Travis. Your friends in high school were delinquents. Mike is a nice guy."

When Maria cleared the table, Mike asked Travis, "Are you gonna ask if you can stay with me?"

Travis gulped. He couldn't think of an excuse to have a slumber party with a grown man. How would he ask?

Mike smiled. "Tell them we're going fishing up in Tomales Bay."

"Are we?"

Mike shrugged. "We can if you want."

❧

Travis packed a knapsack with a change of clothes. They caught the streetcar to Mike's place. It was a clean, one-room apartment with a galley kitchen. There was no bed in sight.

"Do you have a Murphy bed?" Mike said, "Nah, the closet's so big, I made it my bedroom. Sure enough, there was a full-sized bed inside the large closet.

Travis said, "So this is where the magic happens?"

Mike smiled. "If you call jacking off my monster 'magic,' then I guess you could say so."

Travis put a hand on Mike's shoulder. We can make magic now if you want."

Mike checked his watch. "We should wait a couple of hours for the bridge traffic to clear."

Travis sat on the bed and kicked off his shoes. He pulled his pants down, then his underwear. He lay on his back, perched on the edge of the bed, holding open his inviting asshole for the big brute.

"Shit, hold on. It's stuck." Mike had been so turned on by Travis's mating display that he got his cock stuck in his jeans. After a struggle, his heavy cock swung upward, looking like a baseball bat defying gravity. He grabbed a tub of Crisco from the bedside table, greasing the pole and the hole.

"You ready?"

Travis nodded vigorously.

Mike stepped forward until his club-like head found its way between the full mounds of flesh. Travis guided the head to the opening, tugging the slippery cock shaft to pull Mike inside. Mike pushed, and the head popped in. The angle of entry was different, being on a raised full-size bed. Travis only needed to twist a little to allow Mike to slip past the rectum. When Mike was fully inside, he planted his hands on either side of Travis and lowered his chest in a modified push-up, planting his lips on Travis. The love energy was powerful. It only took Mike a few minutes before he was building towards orgasm.

Travis played with Mike's titties, causing the electricity between them to surge.

"Oh, fuck, Travis. That feels so fucking great."

Travis realized that only a few weeks earlier, he had been a nervous virgin, afraid of his own shadow. Today his fireman lover was power-fucking him like a slut, and he loved it. The fat meat slid back and forth deep inside him. With the better bed, Travis was able to use his foot to encourage Mike to take longer and longer strokes until he was running the whole length of his cock from hole to guts.

Mike gasped when he pulled out completely. Travis's hole stayed open, twitching like a fish gasping for air. He plunged back inside in one long, smooth stroke until his cock head pushed up in that same spot on Travis's belly. It was all too much.

"Fuck, I'm gonna come!" He stayed buried, letting the moment last. His belly hairs tickled Travis's tiny cock. That was all he needed. His little dick splattered Mike's belly, chest, and chin with warm boy jism.

"Fill me up."

Mike heard the words and obeyed. "You're so fucking sexy! I'm coming!" And he did.

Afterward, Mike threw Travis a towel. "Here, go get cleaned up. We gotta look presentable when we get to the Cove."

Nick's Cove was two hours north of San Francisco on Tomales Bay, a collection of cabins surrounding a bar and restaurant with a long fishing pier. It was a blue-collar resort frequented by men who wanted to escape from their families for some alone time. It was a weekday, so the resort wasn't busy when they arrived. After dropping off their things, they went for a steak dinner at Nick's, the restaurant. The host Nick, a handsome older man with a handlebar mustache, greeted them at the door.

After a delicious dinner, they had a couple of drinks at the bar.

A Santa Rosa cop sat at one end of the bar. He was in his cups, getting belligerent while spouting off to Nick, the owner.

"What is it with these faggots? They're moving into Russian River and driving out all the respectable people."

Nick polished a glass and said nothing.

The cop pointed at Travis and Mike. "I mean, these guys look like a couple of faggots. Do you let fags stay at the Cove?"

Nick threw the glass to the floor. "Joe shut the fuck up. These two guys are heroes - firemen. And even if they were fags, they'd be welcome here. Now shut your goddamn mouth if you don't want me calling the station and reporting your ass."

Joe the cop stood up, ready for a fight. Nick gestured to the cook, who came out from behind the stove with a butcher's knife.

"You're 86'ed, Joe. Get the fuck out."

The policeman shouted, "You're all a bunch of fucking fags!" He staggered to his car but couldn't find his keys. Nick held the keys up so Joe could see them. The policeman weaved as he came back in.

"No, you're sleeping it off."

Joe said, "I ain't sleeping in the car."

Nick shrugged. He pointed North. Take the last cabin at the end. He slammed a key down, and Joe took it, sheepishly wandering up the shoreline.

Nick said, "Sorry about that, boys. Methinks he doth protest too much. I think he might be gay and just doesn't know it. I, on the other hand, know I am." He winked at them.

The confrontation rattled Travis. Nick put a rough, calloused hand on Travis's dainty paw. "Our time will come, don't worry."

The two firemen didn't catch any fish, but they didn't try. They spent the whole next day in the cabin. Travis was so sore, he thought he would never walk right again.

10

THE ELEPHANT WALK

Several months went by. Travis and Mike grew closer, fighting fires side by side, then making love long into the night. Travis was running out of excuses to spend the night at Mike's place. His mother kept asking if they were smoking marijuana. His father didn't notice Travis was gone. Neither parent could have imagined what their son was really doing with him. Their lovemaking was so passionate neighbors in the building complained. For the first few weeks, Travis felt pain when the sex started, like anyone would who was taking a log of liverwurst up their ass. But love and familiarity brought him to a place where it just felt good the whole time. He'd learned to let go and let pleasure take over, drowning out the pain.

Still, it was hard work letting Mike rearrange his guts every night and most mornings. Travis didn't always get enough sleep. Mike rolled over and started snoring as soon as he finished, but Travis had to wait for his insides to adjust once Mike shot his load and pulled out. It kept him awake at night. He asked Mike to stay inside him. He thought he might get more rest with his soft cock holding him open. That backfired; Mike kept getting hard, and they both lost sleep that night, fucking until dawn. Sex at the firehouse was more challenging than at Mike's place. Small mattresses, fire bells, and nosy coworkers had a negative impact on their sex life.

One day after work, Petey said, "We're gonna get lunch at Hot and Hunky Burgers and then grab some beers at The Elephant Walk. Care to join us?"

The five firemen descended on the Castro, proudly wearing their t-shirts and slacks. Firemen were a fantasy for most gay men. Who could resist a hero with a badge?

The Elephant Walk was a tropical-themed bar/restaurant that replaced the pharmacy on the corner of Castro and 18th. It had the best view out the windows of any bar except the Twin Peaks. Palm trees and slow-moving ceiling fans made the place feel like a Humphrey Bogart flick. It could have been a set from Dark Passage. The drinks were plentiful, and the men were soon several drinks deep in their cups.

As the sun went down, the men began to pair off with admiring young gay men. Keith stumbled out with a wispy young blond man with green eyes. French Fry met a big black man with shoulders wider than the door frame. Even Petey found a daddy's boy to escort him out of the bar. Mike and Travis sat awkwardly, aware of the intense electricity that crackled in the air between them.

Mike said, "I'd like to take you back to my flat and fuck you senseless."

Travis looked up from his drink. "I'd like that."

Together, they stumbled out of the bar onto the street. Travis accidentally bumped into a passerby. The man looked at him and said, "Watch it, faggot." It was Travis's father.

The mood went south quickly.

"What the fuck were you two doing in that bar? That's a fag bar!"

Mike said, "We prefer the term 'gay bar,' sir."

Travis lied. "We didn't know. We just went to get a drink."

Fritz scowled. "That's a load of horse shit, and you know it. The bar is right smack in the middle of fagtown. Are you a fag?"

Mike put a hand on Travis's father's shoulder. "Sir, your son is gay, if that's what you're asking. And we're lovers."

His father spat on the ground. "You ain't never coming home, Travis, you hear me? You're not my son. And you, Mike, you fucking pervert. You ate my wife's cooking, and you're fucking my son? You're a goddamn Judas. That's what you are."

Mike put his arm tightly around Travis and said to him, "This day was coming. Don't freak out." To Travis's father, he said, "Sir, if that's how you feel, then you never loved your son."

Fritz glared at Mike. "If I'd have known he was gonna turn queer, then I would have sent him to the orphanage." He turned to Travis. "You disgust me. Both of you!" He stormed off, cursing at every gay person he saw.

Travis broke away and ran down the street in tears. Mike ran after him. He found him crying into his hands on a stoop.

Travis saw Mike approaching and said, "Get the fuck away. You ruined my life!"

Mike held his hands up. "Hey, hey now. You're freaked out. Your father was a dick to you. Don't push me away. I love you, buddy."

He didn't know why the words came out, but Travis said, "Fuck off, faggot."

Mike didn't leave. He sat down next to Travis, who scooted away from him. They sat together in silence. Mike said, "You can live with me until we find a place."

Travis turned crimson with rage. "Don't you get it? I

don't have a home to go back to now! You told my dad, and now I'm never gonna see my parents again."

Mike looked at the sky, saying, "Time will tell if that's true. We don't know what's in store. Things have a way of sorting themselves out."

Travis was overcome with too many emotions and broke down sobbing again. This time, he put his head on Mike's shoulder. Mike ran his fingers through his lover's hair. Travis stroked Mike's big arm. "At least I won't have to make up excuses to my folks about staying at your place."

Mike chuckled. "You have a home to go back to; it's just not the one you're used to."

Travis raised his head and looked deeply into Mike's eyes. "Do you really mean it?"

Mike nodded. "We're a good fit, Travis. It's rare when two people find each other. You're new to love. I've been with a few guys, and it's never been this good."

Travis wiped his eyes. "It's hard work, but I love it. Getting fucked, I mean."

Mike smiled. "Yeah, it's a lot easier for me, I know, but I've seen your face when I'm buried deep inside you. You love it."

Travis sighed. "Yeah, I do."

"Come on, let's go to my place. We can take a cab."

⚙

Travis turned on the TV back at the flat and flopped on the sofa. His mind raced; he couldn't pay attention to the stupid sitcom. It was some awful show that would be canceled after one season anyway.

Mike made tea. They'd had enough booze already. They sat on the sofa, sipping their tea.

Travis put a hand on Mike's thigh, squeezing the monster stuffed down his pant leg. Mike tore off his shirt and yanked his pants down. He embraced Travis, tonguing his mouth like he could find gold bullion in there. Travis yielded, unbuttoning his shirt and leaning back on a pillow propped against the arm of the couch. Mike unbuttoned Travis's pants, yanking them off and tossing them on the floor. He pulled Travis's underwear down, exposing the beautiful round rump.

"I wanna fuck you so bad."

Travis smiled. "Do it."

Mike rubbed Vaseline inside Travis's butthole, then used his oily hands to grease up his cock. It took a few more dabs in the jar to get it slick enough to fuck. He spit in his hand and wiped it on the head. It reflected the glare of the overhead light, a shiny, slippery knob.

"You ready?" Mike held it against Travis's hole.

Travis nodded.

The older fireman pushed against the opening and was surprised at how easily it slipped inside.

Travis saw the surprise. He wasn't sure why, but coming out to his father had allowed him to relax more than ever before. Mike pushed forward, filling Travis, then popped past the junction. He said, "Goddamn, Travis, you're not too tight anymore. It feels fucking terrific."

Travis was in ecstasy and said nothing in return. He crossed his ankles behind Mike's butt and pulled him closer until, at last, the pubic bone came in contact with Travis's rump. "Fuck me, Mike."

Mike was gentle. He knew Travis was dealing with traumatic family shit. He was surprised when Travis said, "Harder, fuck me good."

Mike picked up his pace, but it wasn't fast enough for the younger man. Travis used his crossed ankles to set the pace, forcing Mike in and out at a breakneck speed. He hurt inside, but he didn't care. Mike could fuck away any pain.

Mike was sure he was hurting Travis. He felt his

cock catching in different places because he was going too fast. He tried to slow down, but Travis kept insisting. Mike had to admit it felt good to fuck with wild abandon. It was the first time he'd pounded anyone this hard in years. The last time he had been so rough, it ended badly. He was worried it would happen again.

"Oh god, Mike, punish me with your giant cock!" Travis was wild with desire. He thrashed and flailed, oblivious to any pain building inside him. Without warning, he sprayed a load of cum all over the sofa pillows.

Mike was in such a frenzy, and it put him over. He thrust as deep as he could, over and over, and came.

As Mike thrusted, Travis became aware of a deep, unnatural pain. It wasn't the pain of being stretched. It felt like an injury.

"Mike, I think I'm hurt."

Mike was still in his head, pounding away, milking the last drops of cum from his massive pole.

Travis hit him on the chest. "Stop. I'm hurt."

The sudden protest startled Mike. "What?"

"I did something wrong."

Mike looked down and saw blood on his cock. When he pulled it out, dark red blood ran out of Travis's backside. The boy grew pale.

"Oh shit, no, not again." Mike called 911.

11

HOLD YOUR BREATH

Travis awoke in the hospital. He was surprised to see his mother by his bedside.

"Mamma?"

"Oh, Travis. I was so worried. Mike called, and I came right down. What happened?"

Mike wasn't in the room. He had no idea what Mike had told her. "I don't remember. What did the doctor say?"

"Oh, he just said you were injured. I keep asking, but he says nothing."

"What did Dad say?" Travis was fishing for information.

"Your father he didn't come home before I got the call."

Travis groaned. He would have to come out to his mother, but this wasn't how he wanted to do it.

"Where's Mike?"

She answered. "He's in the waiting room. You want I should get him?"

"Please."

Mike came in, trying to disguise his guilty face. Travis said, "Mike, I don't remember what happened. And Dad isn't here because he didn't come home. What do I do?"

Mike understood immediately. "Tell your Mom about us."

Mrs. Baumholt looked at Travis. "Tell me what?"

Travis said, "Mom, me and Mike are, well, we're gay. We're in love."

She frowned. "Oh, Dio mio! You think I didn't know?"

Travis sat up, then winced in pain. He fell back onto the bed.

His mother said, "Is it your appendix?"

Travis nodded. "Yeah, I think so." There was no way she was ready for the truth. He wasn't about to say, "Well, Mamma, Mike has a massive dick, and he injured me inside when he fucked me." That would make her pass out. The appendix seemed like a good cover.

She said, "You could have died."

Travis said, "I guess so. I'm really lucky." He looked at Mike, who was bright red with embarrassment and shame. "I'm so lucky Mike is in my life. He saved me."

Mrs. Baumholt turned to hold Mike's hand. "Thank you for saving my son. What's wrong?"

Mike shook his head. "I, uh, I just...yeah. You're welcome. I love your son." He gave Travis a sheepish look.

Travis's mother stroked Mike's hand. "You don't have to be ashamed. His father won't like it, but I just want Travis to be happy."

Mike was a big strong guy, so it looked funny to see tears streaming down his chiseled face. "His father just found out."

Travis said, "He says I can't come back. I'm not welcome home."

"Menaggia sozzo! He's a fool. I tell you what, Travis. I won't cook for him until he changes his mind. He'll cave fast."

Travis shrugged. "I don't want to see him anymore."

His mother gently slapped his face. "You don't mean

that. I can imagine what he said. I know how he is. He'll come around; just wait."

Mike said, "In the meantime, we're shacking up."

❧

TRAVIS NEEDED STITCHES IN HIS COLON. HE HAD TO stay off solid foods for a week. He got paid sick time from the fire station. He worried Mike would get an even better bunk mate and leave him. When he confessed his fears to Mike, the hunky fireman just laughed.

"You are one in a million. No, one in a billion. You got nothing to worry about."

Travis spent time recovering in Mike's small bed. He had to wait a while before having sex again. The doctor, a gay man himself, explained that once the wound area scarred over, it would be stronger than before the injury. They could go back to having sex. Maybe not quite as vigorously, but they could still have a go in a few weeks.

In the meantime, Mike got to enjoy the pleasures of oral sex. One night, Travis lay on the bed, his head dangling, mouth open. Mike entered him, always astonished that he fit. Travis unhooked his jaw and opened his throat, letting Mike into his esophagus. Mike sighed, overjoyed at the sensation of his cock surrounded by the slippery wet gullet. Travis used his throat muscles to swallow more of Mike, pulling him into his mouth further and further until his pubic hair tickled his nose.

"God, Travis, how do you do that?"

There was no way Travis could answer. He could scarcely hum; Mike's enormous cock blocked his throat entirely.

"Mmmph"

Mike pulled back, and Travis exhaled and inhaled

through his nose before pulling Mike to him. He gagged and retched, but he kept it together. When Travis tried to pull away a second time, Mike held his head and forced his way down his throat. Travis had scarcely caught his breath, and now Mike was blocking his airway. He held on until the room turned red, then he patted Mike's leg. Mike released Travis, who let the massive cock drop out of his mouth while he took precious breaths.

Mike said, "We can stop if this is too much."

Travis shook his head. He grabbed the cock head and quickly swallowed the beast again. The blow job continued for thirty minutes. Travis let Mike bring him to the edge of unconsciousness over and over. The more he choked, the more his tiny penis leaked. His undershorts were soaked.

Then Travis tasted the tangy, salty precum that signaled Mike was close.

Mike picked up the pace. "Oh, shit! Oh, man!"

Travis took one huge breath and held it so that Mike could fuck his throat deep. Mike stared, fascinated, watching his cock stretch Travis's throat. The Adam's apple bobbed up and down with each thrust.

Travis surprised himself. His esophagus began to throb. It was as if he had a prostate gland in there somewhere. Maybe it was his lymph nodes, but he was sure he was having a throat orgasm.

"What the fuck! That feels so fucking good!" Mike was startled by the sensation of being stroked by the spasms in Travis's throat.

Travis surprised himself. The thrill of Mike's huge cock deep in his gullet, combined with the strange vibrations in the muscles, caused Travis to shoot a load in his underwear. Mike saw the spreading stain. It put him over the edge.

"Oh, fuck! Here it comes."

He pulled Travis by the ears as he thrust forward, so

far down Travis's throat that the boy didn't need to swallow. The rich cum just flowed right down to his stomach. Travis thrashed from the combination of ejaculation, throat orgasm, and near loss of consciousness. He loved it. Then the room went dark.

The next thing Travis knew, Mike was gently slapping him on the cheek. "Hey, hey, man. Are you okay?"

Travis spoke. It came out in a hoarse whisper. "I've never been better. That was amazing, man."

Mike laughed and hugged Travis to his massive pecs. Travis wanted to keep sucking on Mike, so he put a nipple in his mouth and nursed.

Mike's cock throbbed and lifted from his thighs, poking Travis in the side.

Mike said, "Whoa! You keep that up, and we'll have to do it all over. And this time, it will take a lot longer!"

Travis lifted off the nipple. "Let's do it!"

12

ALL IN A DAY'S WORK

Travis was so thrilled sucking off Mike that he almost liked it more than getting fucked. But he yearned to feel that full sensation in his colon. Mike was a powerhouse, energizing Travis with every blow job, but he fell short of his potential while waiting for the doctor to okay anal sex again.

The day Travis got the all-clear was the morning he and Mike reported for their 24-hour shift at the station. A call came in as soon as they arrived. It was a huge fire that spread from one Victorian house to an Edwardian apartment building. Families were trapped, and the many engines that came had their work cut out for them.

Travis and Mike were pulled off hose duty to go inside and rescue a family trapped on the second floor of the apartment. The stairway was filled with smoke. They rushed up the stairs, past flames on the banister that quickly spread to the steps. They both knew the only way out would be a window.

The family of five cowered in the front room with the window open. A boy lay unconscious. Travis removed his oxygen mask and revived the child while Mike used a portable extinguisher to extinguish fast-spreading flames. The parents and the eldest son went down the ladder alone while Mike threw the daughter over his shoulder. Travis was an expert at holding his breath now. He kept the oxygen mask on the boy, who was still suffering from smoke inhalation and needed all the oxygen he could get.

Travis threw the boy over one shoulder and descended the ladder. When he was halfway down, the whole living room exploded. Flames shot out of the window. He had narrowly avoided a disaster. When he got down, he gazed up at the flames, only to see an elderly woman leaning out of the third-floor window.

"Help! It's just me; somebody help!"

Travis shouted, "Raise the ladder!" It barely reached the third floor. The woman was too feeble to climb out the window, so Travis rushed up and helped her. She was terrified to descend the ladder.

"Hurry! It's gonna blow!"

She said, "I can't. I'm not strong enough."

Travis held her by the waist, carrying her down like a rag doll. He set her down on a ledge because she was too faint to stand. Paramedics rushed to assist her.

He turned to see the family he'd helped rescue. The mother took his hand.

"Thank you for saving Charlie. He's asthmatic and..." She couldn't continue. Her breath grew shallow, and tears came down her cheeks. She grabbed Travis and held him to her. "The world is a better place with you in it. You're a hero."

Travis hadn't felt maternal warmth in weeks. He nearly cried thinking about his mother, who had to reject him to stay in the good graces of his bigot of a father.

She let go of Travis and turned to Mike. "You, too. Both of you are heroes, and I'll never forget your bravery."

Mike shrugged. "All in a day's work, ma'am."

❧

By the time the fire was out, it was dark. The crew returned to the firehouse, starving. French Fry said, "Travis, you worked harder than the rest of us. I'll make spaghetti."

Travis quickly said, "I'm good. I'll cook."

French Fry looked hurt when the whole crew burst into laughter. Travis made Penne Bolognese with garlic bread and an Italian salad. The team was silent as they ate the delicious meal.

Mike said, "Travis, when you cook like that, it makes me fall in love with you."

There were groans. Keith mocked them. "Oh, Travis! Ain't no river deep enough!"

Mike didn't give a shit. He held Travis in an embrace, and they kissed. Catcalls and cheers filled the air.

French Fry said, "Well, I guess that's it. He claimed him."

After supper, Travis and Mike went up to bed. Travis stripped and climbed into the bottom bunk, facing the wall, his perky butt exposed for Mike to use. Mike knelt and put his tongue on the bright pink hole. His tongue was wide, and he lubed and loosened Travis until there was a small dark opening each time he withdrew.

"You're out of practice. Are you ready?"

Travis laughed. "I never wanted something so badly."

Mike lubed his cock with Vaseline and put the tip in. Travis couldn't have prepared for how much it hurt. It felt like the first time. But it was that lovely sweet pain that gives way to pleasure. The pain came in waves as Mike leaned into him, but the heavenly shivers of joy were steady.

"Is that okay?"

Travis nodded. Mike turned the bend, entering Travis's sigmoid colon. As Mike went deeper, the pressure at the anus grew more intense. Mike's massive thick cock grew wider and pressed on Travis's prostate. Travis spasmed. The waves of anal orgasm began. Travis's tiny penis leaked juice like a faulty faucet. It stained the bedsheets.

"Do it, Mike, fuck me!"

Mike pressed harder until his hips met Travis's backside. He pushed harder, and the tip of his cock hit the descending colon. Travis shook with ecstasy.

Mike gingerly pulled back and thrust again.

Travis grunted. "Harder!"

"I don't want to hurt you!"

Travis said, "Don't worry. I know now when it's too much. I'll warn you."

Mike still fucked with less energy than he had in the past. Travis reached back and pulled Mike to him, then pushed. Then he pulled. Faster and faster, Mike's thrusts grew in intensity.

Mike said, "I want to look in your eyes." He pulled back enough to rotate Travis until he faced Mike, his ankles by his ears.

This position was so intimate it allowed Mike to push even further, so he hit the descending colon wall with force.

Travis's eyes rolled up into his head. "Fuck me, Mike."

Mike was getting more comfortable. He took longer, harder strokes. Each thrust hit the magic spot that caused Travis to squirm on the inside.

The boy said, "Oh, fuck, Mike. You're making me come like a woman."

That turned Mike on. His cock swelled, stretching the colon walls and pressing hard on Travis's prostate. His little penis became a sprinkler, spraying both men with a massive load of cum. When it subsided, the itty bitty cock continued to leak clear, seminal fluid.

Mike said, "You come like a man and like a woman."

Travis said, "Maybe I'm part woman. I mean, my cock is like a clit, right?"

Mike liked this dirty talk. He said, "You're my little bitch. Just a little girl."

That was a magic moment. Travis realized he liked being a girly man with a little penis. "Keep saying it."

Mike said, "You got a tight little cunt, but it's deep as fuck."

Travis moaned. "I'm a little cunt."

Mike was so excited he passed the point of no return. "Oh, fuck, Travis. You're my sissy bitch! Daddy's gonna knock you up!"

With those words, Travis came a second time. "Oh yes, Daddy, fuck your little girl." See, you're making me pregnant." Travis put a hand on the belly lump created by Mike's huge thick cock.

"Oh shit, you've got a bun in your oven!"

Mike couldn't stop. He pounded so hard that Travis put a hand on his thigh. "Easy."

Mike heard him and dialed it back half a notch.

Travis said, "Perfect. Oh god, Daddy. You're gonna get your little girl pregnant!"

And that was it. Mike loosed a flood of sperm in Travis's belly. His cock was lodged so deep that the lump in Travis's abdomen grew with each load of cum that filled and stretched him. Travis rubbed the belly with both hands. Mike's sweat dripped onto the stretched tummy. He collapsed on top of Travis, hugging him close.

Mike said, "I'm the luckiest man in the world."

Travis smiled. "And I'm the luckiest little girl."

They both laughed. They held each other, and Mike stayed hard enough to remain inside Travis while they gently drifted off to sleep.

EPILOGUE

The two firemen were hailed as heroes in the paper the next day. Like Greek soldiers on the battlefield, their love drove them to do more heroic deeds in the months and years to come. Everybody knew they were gay, and nobody gave a shit because they saw how strong their bond made them. In every fire, Mike and Travis were always the first picks when someone needed rescuing. They were frequently woken out of sleep at Mike's place when a fire was so destructive that they were the only two who could perform the rescue. They didn't mind. Working side by side was reward enough. The overtime pay paid for their little getaways to Nick's Cove to do a little "fishing" on weekends.

Their savings grew, and they eventually bought a two-bedroom house on 20th near Noe, two steep blocks from the bars on Castro Street. Eventually, they persuaded Travis's father and mother to visit their home and enjoy a home-cooked meal. His dad was gruff, and uncomfortable, but he apologized.

"You're my son. I don't understand why you like men, but if you do, I'm glad it's Mike."

Mike beamed. Travis wiped a tear from his eye. His

mother breathed a sigh of relief. They lived out their days in harmony, fighting fires together until they were old and rich enough to retire. They still live up there in their little house. Go ahead and knock on their door; they love visitors.

ABOUT PETER SCHUTES

Peter Schutes is a fictional character. He was modeled after the gay pulp fiction authors of the 1970s and 1980s. His creator often wondered who the men were who wrote these books, and so he created Peter to satisfy his curiosity.

Peter was born in 1896 to a wealthy New England family. His whole life, he carried a massive burden: he had a gigantic penis. His sex life was defined by the men who worshipped him.

Peter led a tempestuous life, which is documented in the fictional masterpiece "The Autobiography of Peter Schutes." To learn more about this prolific and prodigious author, we recommend reading his immortal tale of life with too much of a good thing.

OTHER BOOKS FROM PETER SCHUTES PUBLISHING

E-books and Paperbacks (as noted)

The Able Seaman

The Anaconda Copper

The Autobiography of Peter Schutes*

Backwoods Delivery

Big Bodies of All Sizes*

Big Hole River*

Bobbing Buoys and Salty Seamen*

Bunkhouse Buddies*

The Butt Baby*

Cloistered

Confessions of a Rodeo Clown*

Dark as a Dungeon*

Demonic Deception *aka* Deceived, Cursed & Blessed

Desert Island Daddies

The Expectant Member

Firehouse Lovers

The Fish

Five Erotic Tales*

The Gospel of Priapus*

Hercules and Lippos

Hobo Honey

Hotshot

Logger's Delight

Muscle Bottom*

Panama Heat

Satanic Seductions*

Satan's Sissy Boy

The Slaves of Rome*

The Thigh Baby

Under the Boardwalk

World's Biggest

Coming Soon

Backwoods Delivery - The Complete Daddy's Boy Series

Like the Greeks Do*

Higher Education*

Hoboes, Hustlers, and Jailbirds*

Small Cockpits and Big Hangars*

Tales of Two Daddies*

*Available as Paperbacks

9 781963 667004